THOMA[illegible]

Thomasina Unsworth was born in Athens in 1968. She trained as an actor at the Royal Central School of Speech and Drama and spent the following decade working extensively in theatre and television.

She began teaching by chance when she was seven months pregnant with her first child and was asked to do some private coaching. Her life changed course as she discovered a fascination with the process of unlocking the actor, and facilitating their explorations. A degree in English Literature and a Masters in Theatre Practices followed, as did much coaching and time spent with companies as a workshop leader. She has continued to develop her ideas, eschewing rigid methodologies and focusing instead on the various and multiple needs of the individual artist.

She is now Head of First Year on the Acting and Actor Musicianship courses at Rose Bruford College. Her first book *Becoming an Actor* is also published by Nick Hern Books.

She lives in Brighton with her husband and two daughters, Isobel and Esme.

drama games

A series of books for teachers, workshop leaders, directors and actors in need of new and dynamic activities when working in education, workshop or rehearsal.

Also available in this series
DRAMA GAMES FOR...

Chris Johnston
THOSE WHO LIKE TO SAY NO

Jessica Swale
CLASSROOMS AND WORKSHOPS
DEVISING
REHEARSALS

Katherine Zachest
YOUNG CHILDREN

The publisher welcomes suggestions for further titles in the series.

Thomasina Unsworth

drama games

FOR ACTORS

Exploring Self, Character and Text

Foreword by Richard Eyre

NHB

NICK HERN BOOKS
London
www.nickhernbooks.co.uk

A Nick Hern Book

DRAMA GAMES FOR ACTORS

First published in Great Britain in 2017
by Nick Hern Books Limited, The Glasshouse,
49a Goldhawk Road, London W12 8QP

Designed and typeset by
Nick Hern Books, London
Printed and bound in Great Britain by
Ashford Colour Press, Gosport, Hampshire

A CIP catalogue record for this book
is available from the British Library

ISBN 978 1 84842 373 2

MIX
Paper from
responsible sources
FSC® C011748

To all my students
over the years

FOREWORD

Most of us have an indecent curiosity about what other people do in private. Sex and tax, for instance: 'What do you do in bed?' and 'How much do you earn?' are the questions that underlie all profile journalism and most biography. My own particular corner of prurience concerns the working habits of directors: I'm inordinately fascinated by what they are. Directors are not very gregarious creatures, at least among their own kind, and if you were to search for a collective noun for them it would probably be a 'solitude'. When we do gather together, we're wary of discussing each other's work, and warier still of asking how it was achieved. Rehearsals are a private province; no one likes to be observed, so it's hard to see enough to imitate, even if you have a model to follow.

Directors are often self-effacing, often surprisingly lacking in the gift and appetite for self-promotion, and, in spite of a high estimation of their own importance, are often reluctant to capitalise on it by making public pronouncements on their craft. It's all the odder therefore that directors occupy such an elevated status in contemporary mythology, often, like conductors, placed somewhere between the maestro and the magus, when in fact they're more like teachers or doctors. If there's one thing I've learned it's that it's better to be more like the pupil or the patient than the teacher or the doctor. The mistake is to pretend that you have all the answers.

Which is one of the reasons that I'm consistently reluctant to recommend my 'process' to any director, and suspicious of any young director who asks to be an assistant of mine in order to learn about it. If I chose to rationalise the way I work I suppose it would amount to a 'process', but it is so idiosyncratic and personal that I wouldn't dignify it with that description.

A rehearsal has to be a time when actors can experiment, invent, explore, discuss, dispute, practise and play, and it is the job of a director to create a world – private and secure – where this activity can go on without fear of failure. There is no method that guarantees a good rehearsal. It's as hard to know why some highly articulate, learned and intelligent directors seem unable to animate a cast of actors, as it is to understand how the same orchestra can be inspired by some conductors but seem commonplace in the hands of others.

If you ask me, 'What do you need to be a director?' I'd have to say this: you need to be somehow assertive and yet self-effacing, to be dogged and yet pliable, to be demanding and yet supportive. And if this sounds like a prescription for a perfect marriage partner, it's because directors are ever hopeful of making a successful marriage of actor and character, of text and design, of play and audience, so perhaps, if they look hesitant, doubtful, and diffident, it's because they know just how difficult it is – as in real life – to make a marriage work.

And if you ask me, 'How do you learn to be a director?' I'd recommend a poem called 'Garden Hints' by Douglas Dunn, which begins with the line: 'Only a garden can teach gardening.' Directing is like that: only working with actors in a rehearsal room can offer a real insight into the craft.

The start of most rehearsals resembles others more than it differs from them. Rehearsals have to begin somewhere – usually it's a meeting of the cast and a reading of the play. The director stands like a heron, rigid with anxiety, talks a little – or a lot, depending on temperament – and his or her words drift like incense over a group of actors who, regardless of their mutual familiarity, are united only in their nervous anticipation and social unease. It never works to give the actors – who are always numbed to deafness by nerves – a lengthy lecture about the background to the play and its meaning: it doesn't encourage actors to be made to feel that the director holds all the cards and they hold none.

So how do you start rehearsals? It's always a problem: how do you get a disparate set of individuals to work as an ensemble within a few days? British actors are good at this, but you still have to find means of mutual familiarisation, ways in which they can legitimately sniff each other out. I change my approach for each production. Sometimes we just sit around a table and I encourage everyone, regardless of experience and size of part, to talk about the play, about their parts, about themselves. Sometimes we do physical and vocal exercises. Sometimes we do improvisations connected with the play. And sometimes we even play games – and many of them are in this book. Thomasina Unsworth gives you a mass of invaluable ideas for drama exercises for all ages and all types of actors, amateur or professional. It's hard to imagine anyone involved in theatre who wouldn't find it useful.

Richard Eyre

Richard Eyre is a theatre, opera, television and film director and writer. He was Artistic Director of the National Theatre from 1988 to 1997, where his productions included Guys and Dolls, Richard III, King Lear, Racing Demon, Skylight, The Invention of Love *and* Vincent in Brixton. *His other theatre work includes* Amy's View, Mary Poppins, Private Lives, Betty Blue Eyes, Mr Foote's Other Leg, *and his own versions of* Hedda Gabler, Ghosts *and* Little Eyolf. *His films include* Tumbledown, Iris, Notes on a Scandal, Henry IV, Parts 1 and 2 *and* The Dresser. *He has published four books, including* National Service, *a journal of his time at the National, which won the Theatre Book Prize. He has received many awards for theatre, television and film, was knighted in 1997, and became a Companion of Honour in 2017.*

CONTENTS

PART ONE

SELF

The aim of Part One is to provide tools for actors to develop their ability to relax, focus, concentrate, imagine, and to work as a group. These exercises are collected together here because they can be explored without reference to either character or text. Some are simply about having fun and getting energised; others will require connection on a much deeper level.

The exercises are ordered in such a way that they begin with solo explorations, move on to work done in pairs, and then to games involving a group.

Solo Work

Circles of Attention

Lie on the floor on your back. Make sure you are warm before you start, as you will be in this position for some time.

Feel the weight of the floor beneath you, supporting you. As you lie there, allow yourself to feel relaxed, but remain alert so that if someone clapped their hands you would be ready to jump up and run around the room. Notice how you are feeling. Note any points of tension in your body. Are your hands clenched? Is your neck locked? Isolate the areas of tension and ease them out.

Be aware of your breathing. Allow the breath to come in and out in an easy, wave-like motion. Just as the tide drives the wave and draws it back, so your breath enters and leaves your body without you having to force it.

Listen to the sounds that your body makes. Acknowledge your physical presence in the space.

Without losing the sense of yourself in the room, listen to other noises that you might be able to hear. Are the pipes creaking? Can you hear the ticking sounds coming from the strip lighting above you? A room is full of sounds; we just need to give ourselves time to listen to them.

If your mind wanders don't get cross with yourself, because that is a distraction that will lead to tension. Just gently return your focus to all those noises pulsing through the room.

Now allow yourself to take in sounds coming from outside of the room, but in its immediate vicinity. Can you hear voices? Are the leaves on the trees rustling in the wind? Did you notice a door slamming nearby?

Imagine that the space around you is like an elastic band that can expand or decrease according to your will. Expand the elastic band of your imagination and listen to noises from further away. Can you hear a baby's first cry from the local hospital? Can you hear a couple arguing in a parked car a few streets away? If your mind wanders, gently bring it back.

Now expand that band of imagination further still. You can listen to anything you want in the world: your mother singing to herself from behind a closed bathroom door; oil wells dripping in Texas; skis cutting through hard snow. You can hear anything at all that your imagination cares to focus on. All you have to do is listen.

Now expand that band even further. What does it sound like in space? Does the air hum with thick silence? Do meteorites smash noisily into each other? Do stars have an electric sound? Allow yourself to float through space, listening to all the extraordinary sounds that you can imagine.

Gently bring yourself back through all the stages of listening, allowing that band to shrink towards you until you are back in the room again, listening to your own breathing and heartbeat. Notice any changes, physically or emotionally, that you might be experiencing.

Time	Skills
15	*Focus, Imagination, Relaxation*

Breath

Lie on the floor on your back.

To begin with, simply inhale for a count of four and then release that breath for a count of four. Both the inhalation and exhalation should be done through your nose rather than your mouth.

Once you have established this pattern of breath put one hand on your chest and the other on your belly. Take a deep breath in through the nose. As you do so, check that it is your diaphragm that expands and not your chest. Having one hand on each area will help you to notice what is happening to you physically and to make any adjustments necessary. Begin to establish a pattern where you take six to ten breaths per minute. Continue this simple process for ten minutes.

Now sit up and put your right thumb over your right nostril. Inhale deeply through your left nostril. When you have inhaled fully, place your right ring finger over your left nostril and release your thumb, now exhale through your right nostril. Continue this for ten minutes, inhaling through the left nostril and exhaling through the right.

Stand up and take a long, slow breath full of air through your nose. Follow this immediately with a quick strong exhale that is initiated from deep in your belly.

When you have established this pattern, speed the process up so that you are inhaling and exhaling through your nose every couple of seconds. Do a total of ten breaths in this way.

Remaining standing, now close your eyes and concentrate on tightening and relaxing each muscle group for two or three seconds at a time. Start with your feet, not forgetting your toes, move up through your knees, thighs, buttocks, chest, hands, arms, neck, jaw and right up into your eyes. All the time you should maintain a steady flow of deep, slow breaths, in and out through your nose. Make sure that, as you stand there, you are not slumping in your body, or straining by lifting your chin too high.

Note

This series of exercises should be done in a room that is neither too hot nor too cold. If you have a blocked nose, blow it before you start. If you are asthmatic, be careful as the continual deep breathing could provoke your asthma.

Time	Skills
30+	*Breathing, Focus, Relaxation*

Rays of Energy

Close your eyes and begin to ease the tension out of your body starting with your feet and working up to the top of your head.

As you begin to relax, feel your breath moving through your body.

Visualise your breath as energising, warm, yellow sunlight. As you breathe in, see the light travelling from the very top of your head down to your toes. As you exhale, reverse the direction of the flow of light, so that it begins in your toes and journeys up to the top of your head.

Continue to relax, feeling the breath through your whole body, and as you inhale, imagine that your inward breath is absorbing the energy from the surrounding room.

As you exhale, send that energy back so that it reaches the furthest corner of the room from where you are standing.

Now, making sure that you have some distance from anyone or anything around you, raise your arms so that the palms of your hands are facing outward. Inhale energy and then exhale it, imagining as you do so that your breath is coming from your outstretched palms. Direct the energy of that breath to someone or something else in the room.

Repeat the process until you have established the flow of energy in and out of you. Maintain your visualisation of warm, yellow sunlight as you inhale and exhale.

Time	Skills
10+	*Energy, Relaxation*

Centres of Energy

Make sure that you are warm enough. You will be still for some time. Lie on the floor on your back, close your eyes and still your thoughts.

Picture yourself on a warm, sandy beach. The sand beneath you is soft, but it is also firm enough to support you.

Allow your head to sink into this soft sand and feel its warmth radiate through your body. It seeps across your shoulders, down your back, along your arms, elbows and hands. Feel the warmth in your buttocks, down the length of your legs into your heels and through to your toes. Lie for a few moments enjoying this warmth, and as you do so pay attention to your breathing. Think of your breathing as a wave. Without apparent effort the tide goes in and out – it is the same with your breath. Breathing should be an easy, natural process.

Focus on the base of your spine and imagine that you can see a vibrant red glow of energy gently rotating there. This is the root or base centre, your connection with the earth. Think of this as your sense of identity, your sense of self. Spend some time infusing that red glow with ever-brighter colour and intensity as it rotates in the base of your spine. Feel an increasing sense of self.

Move your focus to your lower abdomen and now imagine that there is a bright globe of orange energy there. This is your creative centre, your sexual centre. Spend time paying attention to this area and keep infusing the globe with a vivid orange colour.

Now shift your focus to your solar plexus, which is the knot of nerve endings housed between your stomach and your spine. Think of this as your emotional centre and spend time picturing a yellow sphere swirling and massaging that knot of nerve endings.

The centre of your chest is your heart centre. Picture a vibrant, emerald-green sphere swirling right in the middle of your ribcage. Infuse the heart centre with green light and allow it to radiate from your body.

Next, focus on your throat, your communication centre. When we are blocked, emotionally or creatively, the blockage is often manifested in a constriction of our vocal cords. Now imagine your throat opening and fill it with an intense, sky-blue colour. Picture a sky-blue swirling sphere of energy massaging your vocal cords.

Your forehead houses your third eye and is the centre for clairvoyance. You use this centre to develop a sense of alertness, which enables you to be almost ahead of the moment that you are in. This is a powerful centre as it is one step away from your subconscious. Spend some time investing this centre with a vibrant violet energy.

Now you have reached the top of your head, or your crown centre. Focus your attention there and imagine that the top of your head is opening up, letting a stream of light come pouring in. This centre is infused with ultraviolet light, and through it we communicate with the universe.

Imagine that this stream of light is cascading down your body. As it descends, it ignites the violet light in the middle of your forehead; passing through the sky-blue energy in your throat; through the emerald-green heart centre and lighting it up; as it passes down through the emotional centre in the solar plexus, which resonates with yellow energy; then down to the creative centre in your lower abdomen, lighting the orange sphere there; and travelling finally down to the base of your spine, where the red sphere grounds you and connects all your energy centres, right the way up your spine.

Take a moment for that utter sense of who you are to settle in you; your personality, your creative energy, your emotions, your capacity for love, your ability to communicate, your spontaneous response to sound and action, and your higher consciousness, which keeps everything integrated and open.

When you are ready, gradually bring yourself back imaginatively to that warm beach and the imprint of your body in the sand. Finally, bring your focus back to your own breath. Notice any changes in the nature of your breathing. Notice how your body now feels in the space.

Slowly roll over on to one side, then come up to a standing position, only raising your head at the very end of the movement.

Note

This exercise might initially feel strange. It may be that the idea of centres of energy sends you running for the hills. However, if you persevere you may well find that you begin to feel more energised, present and open. Do the exercise over regular periods of time in order to gain a fuller understanding of it. You may find that the response is greater in certain areas of your body than others. This provides you with an interesting insight into the way you operate, and where you might struggle to find connection and release. It is something that should be practised; it may well not have a universally powerful effect immediately.

Time	Skills
30+	*Energy, Focus, Imagination, Relaxation*

Pair Work

Receiving and Responding

Stand facing your partner, with a comfortable distance between you.

Each of you inhales deeply through your nose and exhales through your mouth. Gradually allow yourselves to find a common rhythm so that you are breathing in and out in unison.

Once this has been established, alter the rhythm so that as one player inhales, the other is exhaling. Allow this alternating pattern of breath to exist between you for some time.

As you exhale, extend your arms towards your partner as if you were offering them your breath. As your partner exhales, draw your arms in towards your chest as though you are gathering their breath to you. The gestures of reaching out and drawing in should be continuous and fluid.

After a while you can begin to make a sound on your exhalation. It doesn't need to be beautiful! Exchange sounds with each other.

You can begin to play with volume and pitch. Allow this play to reflect what your partner's sound is making you feel. Respond to each other and a dialogue of noise will ensue. Avoid trying to be too literal: you are not mimicking an actual conversation with words, but rather responding on a quite basic level to your partner as their sound reaches you.

Allow yourselves to experience this exchange before gradually decreasing your volume until you are both back to the earlier alternation of breath. Allow your gestures to become smaller and smaller until you stop the movements altogether.

Finally, return to your own breathing pattern. Notice any reactions, physical and emotional, that you have to the exercise.

Time	**Skills**
15	*Awareness, Breathing, Collaboration, Focus*

Mirroring

Face your partner. You can sit or stand in front of each other.

Label yourselves A and B. Player A commits to a slow and clear movement. For example, he or she reaches up with their left arm.

Player B should copy this precisely and the movement will be repeated between both players until Player A decides to change it. Now A might slowly extend both arms outwards in a gesture that is wide and open. B will copy this and the movement will continue until Player A decides to change it.

Maintain eye contact at all times, and make sure that the movements are simple and clear. You can use music during this exercise and, if you do, it can influence the gestures that you choose.

Once this process has been established, you should arrive at a situation where neither player initiates the movement. Each of you mirrors the other person, but in such a way that anyone observing would be unable to tell which player is moving and which is copying. It should simply flow between you, changing organically as you become increasingly in tune with the person opposite you.

You can move around, but you must not lose eye contact. You should never over-complicate what you are doing so that your partner is unable to mirror you accurately – you are not trying to catch the other person out!

+ Music (optional)

Time	Skills
15+	*Awareness, Collaboration, Control, Responsiveness*

Communicating Without Words

Stand opposite your partner with enough space between you to be separate, but not so far away that you are striving to observe what the other person is doing. Label yourselves A and B.

You should not engage with this exercise in a literal way. You are going to communicate with your partner, but you are not attempting to create a logical dialogue between you.

Without any planning, Player A begins to focus all their attention on one part of their body. It could be a foot, an arm, a knee; it is not important where they put their focus, only that they then give that area their full attention.

As a result of this narrow focus, Player A will experience an impulse to move. Without any premeditation and as soon as they feel that impulse they must act on it. For example, if they have been focusing on their right hand, they may have an impulse to clench their fist, or offer up their palm, or extend their fingers. Again, it is not important what the impulse is, only that it is fully committed to.

Player B has been focusing on Player A during this time and will have noticed their movement. As a result they will have an impulse to respond physically to what they have seen their partner do. For example, if they have seen Player A clench a fist, then they may have an impulse to raise their left leg in front of them. As you can see, the response is not necessarily a logical one. Instead, both players' body parts are given the freedom to respond and to communicate with each other, without censor or premeditation.

Having observed this second movement, Player A will then have an impulse to respond physically, and so they will in turn trigger a further movement of response in Player B.

Continue the exercise until both of you are communicating freely. This exercise is about using your body responsively in relation to another person's. As you do so, you will become increasingly aware of the space between you – and the energy that is created in it as a result of the mutually responsive communication between two bodies.

If, in the course of the exercise, you find that you have an impulse to make a particular noise, then do so. This in turn will be responded to. However, avoid using specific words or trying to create a rational dialogue.

Note

This is instinctive work, not cerebral. You can discuss any discoveries after you have finished, but while the game is on, there is no need to attach any literal meaning to what you are doing.

Time	Skills
20+	*Awareness, Communication, Focus*

Guarding the Keys

You can play this game with just two players, but it is useful to have other participants to form a circle around the central pair if possible.

The group form a wide circle, inside of which is the playing area. They should sit on the floor, but their role is to act as a safety barrier, preventing active players from straying from the safe space and walking into a wall, chair or other obstacle in their path.

Two players enter the circle, are blindfolded and placed apart from each other. Each of them will be given a rolled-up newspaper, and then they will be turned around on the spot so that they feel disorientated.

Place a set of keys on the floor in front of one of the blindfolded players. They are allowed to touch them in order to locate their whereabouts, but after that they are not allowed to cover them with their hand, or any other body part, for any length of time. This player is the guard of an imaginary castle, and their objective is to prevent anyone from stealing those keys.

The other player is the thief. They don't know where the keys to the castle are – so their objective is to locate and then steal them.

While the rest of the group watch, both players must pursue their objectives. They each have the use of the newspaper and of all their senses except sight. They need to be careful that they don't just lash out randomly. They must sense each other and use strategies to get what they want.

Players might crouch low, placing themselves closer to floor level, and so to the keys. They might not move for a length of time, confusing their opponent with their stillness. They might use their newspaper by rustling it against the floor as far away from themselves as they can, causing their opponent to think that they are elsewhere in the circle, and so disorientating them. They might probe the air around them with the newspaper to ascertain whether the other player is nearby. They might use the newspaper as a deterrent, swiping at the place they think the other player is standing. If they touch each other they might spring apart, but the thief will then have knowledge of where the keys are, and the guard might feel the need to move them.

Sometimes the guard loses a sense of where the keys are, and must then try to relocate them. Simply bashing at each other with the newspapers will not result in anything other than a fruitless duel. In order to grab the keys or to protect them, tactics must be employed. All the time the players must be aware of every slight sound or movement within the circle.

The game ends either when the keys have been successfully snatched, or when the guard has prevented the theft of the keys for a set amount of time.

+ Blindfolds, newspapers and keys

Time	Skills
5+	*Communication, Control, Focus, Goal-seeking*

Communicating the Senses

Begin by looking at a person or an object for thirty seconds. Then, looking away so that you can no longer see that person or object, describe it in detail and with accuracy to your partner. When you have done so, return to your initial point of concentration to see whether your description did it justice, or whether you glossed over much of what is actually there if you are observant.

Now, shut your eyes or use a blindfold. Your partner will give you an object, which you have a minute to explore thoroughly through touch. When your time is up, return the object and then describe to your partner with accuracy and detail what it felt like. Open your eyes and see how precise you were.

Wear the blindfold, or close your eyes again, and focus on what you can smell within the surrounding room. For instance, perfume, coffee, sweat, etc. After two minutes, open your eyes, and with detail and accuracy recall for your partner exactly what you smelled.

Next, spend a minute considering what it is you can taste in your mouth. Did you recently brush your teeth? Are you a smoker? Have you just had a coffee? When your time is up, communicate with detailed accuracy the taste you experienced.

Now try and recall imaginatively a variety of tastes. Choose strong evocative flavours, perhaps lemon or curry or tomato ketchup? Without naming for your partner what you are describing, try and communicate in as much detail as possible the specific taste you have remembered.

Remember the last time you were out in the rain, or watched the sun come up on a beach, or danced to a particular piece of music. You can choose any event that you wish to recall, but your job now is to communicate with as much detail as you can, the feelings you had during the experience. Try and recall your mood at the time in detail. When you have been through all these stages then swap roles with your partner and listen to their experiences.

Note

The key thing is to remember the feelings that the exercise provokes in you, rather than the concrete circumstances of any memories; there is no need to list dates and times, etc.

+ Blindfolds (optional) and objects	
Time	**Skills**
30+	*Awareness, Communication, Focus*

Balancing Your Weight

Stand facing your partner.

Each of you places your hands on the other person's shoulders. Imagine that there is a line in between you, running across your arms. You can physically establish this by placing a strip of tape on the floor between you, or putting an object there.

Now push against each other using your full strength, avoiding crossing over that line between you. If one player does step over then start again. Experience the forces of pressure and of resistance. These sensations will exist in you simultaneously. What reaction does this provoke in you?

Now repeat this exercise, but do so standing back to back, leaning against each other. Use each other's weight and maintain contact throughout. Gradually step away from each other, maintaining that contact through the back. Bend your knees as you do so until you end up, back against back, on the floor.

Continue to push against your partner and try to stand again without placing your hands on the floor. Keep practising until you can make the movement of sitting and rising as fluid as possible.

When you have managed this, sit on the floor with your backs pressing together. Reaching behind you, link arms with your partner. The soles of your feet should be flat on the floor so that you have the maximum support. Obviously your knees will then be bent. Using each other's weight, rise to standing and then lower yourself to sitting as you did previously. If you get confident with this, try alternating the movements, so that one of you rises while the other sits.

An extension of this exercise requires a minimum of three people to participate. Groups of three or four are ideal, but you can increase the number of players further.

The group stands in a circle, facing in, with everyone holding the wrist of the person to the right and left of them. Step backwards until your arms are extended. Your arms should not be locked or taut. Find the balance between you, which will allow everyone to sink down to the floor so that you are all seated, with your soles flat on the floor and your knees bent. From this position, using each other's weight, pull yourselves up to standing. Repeat until the movement is as fluid as possible.

Note

These exercises require a level of trust, as they will only work if you constantly negotiate the balance of the weight between you. One player cannot dominate the process, as each player must be equally responsible for completing the movement.

Time	Skills
15+	*Awareness, Collaboration, Control, Coordination*

Reacting to an Impulse

Stand facing your partner on a diagonal across the room. If you are working as part of a larger group then the rest can observe the exercise, but you should resist any urge you might have to make things 'interesting' for those watching.

Maintain eye contact with your partner throughout this exercise. If you have an impulse to move as a result of observing them, then do so. For example, as you look across the room at the other player you might get a sense that they are welcoming you and so you might walk towards them.

Your partner will be observing your behaviour, and they in turn will respond to what they see, and the impulse that triggers in them. The result of your move towards your partner might be that they feel threatened and so back away. This in turn will trigger a response in you, which you must then act upon without censorship.

Do not try to construct a narrative out of the physical dialogue between you. Your job is to stay present in the moment, responsive to your partner's behaviour, and able to allow your resulting impulses to find expression.

You may discover that your breath alters, and that you want to let out a noise such as a sigh or a laugh. It is fine to release this, but do not use actual words.

Note

You may find that for a long time nothing happens: that is fine. Resist the temptation to inject something *engaging* into the proceedings. Dare to simply keep yourself open and connected to the person opposite you. If you do have an impulse to react in some way, then resist censoring it.

Time	Skills
15+	*Awareness, Communication, Responsiveness,*

Group Work

Three Versions of Tag

First Version: Categorical Tag

Before the game begins, select a category of people, such as film stars or politicians. Each player chooses the name of someone from that category, and lets the rest of the group know what it is. So they might say '*I am Russell Crowe*' or '*I am Margaret Thatcher*'.

Elect a person to be 'it'. His or her job is to tag someone else within the group.

Everyone else must avoid being tagged but the only way of doing this is to call out the chosen name of someone else in the group before being touched – e.g. '*Margaret Thatcher!*' The person who is 'it' must then chase the person whose adopted name is Margaret Thatcher. If you fail to call a name in time and get tagged, then you are out. Remember, when someone goes out their name is no longer available to use in the game.

You must articulate the name you call really clearly.

The game stops when the last player has been tagged.

Second Version: Tissue Tag

Everyone puts a sheet of tissue paper in their back pocket, making sure that the paper is visibly hanging out. If you aren't wearing something with pockets then tuck it into the back of your waistband, but with the same effect.

There is no single player who is 'it' this time. The aim is for everyone to collect as many pieces of tissue as possible, while making sure that their own paper is not swiped, because if that happens they are out of the game. In order to achieve this you must ensure that there is no one behind you, but that you are in a position to get the paper from someone else.

Third Version: Stuck in the Mud

Another version of Tag you might have played is called Stuck in the Mud.

Choose someone to be 'it'. The normal rules of Tag apply, where you must avoid being touched by that player.

However, if you do get tagged, instead of leaving the game you become frozen to the spot – or 'stuck in the mud'. You can't continue playing until one of the other players hugs you. When you have been hugged you are free to continue the game.

You must not stay in an embrace for longer than five seconds, and if you do so, then the player who is 'it' can tag you both and the pair of you will be rooted to the spot.

If the player who is 'it' manages to freeze everyone then the game is at an end.

+ Tissue paper	
Players	**Skills**
10+	*Awareness, Energy*

Go!

The whole group makes a large circle in the room facing inwards, so that everyone can see one another.

One player stands in the centre of the circle holding a ball. When everyone is ready, this player throws the ball to someone standing in the circle. Before it reaches that person another player shouts '*Go!*', whilst intercepting the ball and running into the centre, replacing the player previously standing there. This player then throws the ball towards someone else in the circle before it is intercepted by another player shouting '*Go!*', and running in.

This game continues until a speed and fluidity of playing is established.

Time	Players	Skills
5+	10+	*Energy, Focus*

Chasers and Runners

Everyone is dotted around the room, standing stock-still.

Choose one player to be the runner and another to be the chaser. As is pretty obvious from these job descriptions, the two players do just that – one of them chases and the other runs away.

The chaser pursues the runner, but if the runner stands in front of someone else, with his or her back to that player, then the runner is safe. The person they have stood in front of, however, is not! That person now becomes the runner and is pursued by the chaser. They will only be safe if they manage to stand in front of someone else, facing out with their back to them.

If the chaser catches the runner then the roles are immediately reversed – and the pursuer becomes the pursued.

Time	Players	Skills
10+	10+	*Awareness, Energy*

The Pointing Game

The group begins walking around the room. Whilst doing so, they point to objects they can see and say out loud what they are. For example, point at a window and say '*Window*'; point at a bag and say '*Bag*'.

When this simple task has been established, and everyone is comfortable with it, the rules change a little. The first time players point at something, they don't say what it is out loud, but remember it and then when they point at the next thing, they say the object that they have just stored in their memory.

For example:

- Point at the floor – Silence.
- Point at a chair – '*Floor.*'
- Point at the door – '*Chair.*'
- Point at the ceiling – '*Door.*'

And so on.

As the group find their own rhythm, and become more confident, the game should gradually speed up, so that the players are eventually running as fast as possible, avoiding collision with anyone else. To steer clear of each other they may find that every so often they will need to change direction, or alter their path. This adds to the difficulty of the game as players are being asked to think very quickly about more than one thing at a time.

Time	Skills
5–10	*Energy, Focus*

Mind Games

Everyone gets into groups of four. One group member sits on a chair, another stands to the left of them and a second stands to their right. The fourth player positions themselves opposite, standing facing them.

The player on the left asks a simple general-knowledge question, which the person seated has to answer with the minimum of thinking time.

No sooner have they given an answer than the player on the right asks a basic maths question, which must be answered immediately.

As soon as they have done so, the person standing in front does an action that must be copied accurately by the seated player. For example, they might hand-jive, or tap the top of their head, or punch the air with a fist. The seated player must complete this before they hear another general-knowledge question from the person on their left. So it continues with a circle of questions and actions with no pausing. If the seated player doesn't know the answer to a question they should simply guess and move on.

Each player has five minutes of chair time before swapping places, so everyone takes a turn at being under pressure.

Note

This game should be played at breakneck speed, but remember it is not a test where the seated player is expected to get everything right. Rather it is about actors working and exercising their brains, so that they become mentally alert and present in the room. Everyone involved will have to think quickly to come up with questions and answers, gestures and responses, in rapid succession.

Players	Skills
4+	*Energy, Focus, Responsiveness*

Keeping the Ball Up

This is a very simple game, but the group must come up with the best strategy for playing it effectively.

The aim is to keep a ball up in the air by continually tapping it with the palm of the hand. Players can only tap the ball once at a time, so someone else must touch the ball before they can do so again. Select a player to count the number of taps.

If the ball does drop to the floor there must be no apology made and no blame apportioned. A player simply picks up the ball and the game continues with the counting starting from zero again.

The group should come up with strategies, such as where to position themselves, and whether any system is needed in order for the ball to be kept up in the air for as long as possible.

Note

This is a good game to use with a new group. It helps people to bond in pursuit of a common goal. It also requires focus and awareness of each other. I've played the game with a group whose record was 730 taps before the ball dropped to the floor!

+ A ball		
Time	**Players**	**Skills**
10+	4+	*Awareness, Collaboration, Energy*

Chairs

Place chairs at intervals around the room. These should *not* be equidistant from each other; there should be different-sized gaps between them.

Each member of the group sits on a chair, except one player who must remain standing. There is no chair put out for them.

The aim for those occupying the chairs is to swap places with another person without losing their seat to the player who is standing. That player is on the hunt for their own chair to sit on, and as soon as anyone vacates a seat then it becomes available to steal. See how many exchanges can be made before the player without a seat secures one. Each seated player should attempt to move a minimum of five times.

An essential rule is that if someone goes to move then they must commit to that action. They cannot stand up and then hastily sit down again when they see that they are not safe to swap. As far as possible, play this game in silence.

Note

This game requires a great deal of concentration, and all players must be aware of each other at all times. Collectively the group is working to outwit the player without a chair. In order to do this, non-verbal communication must be strong between players.

+ Chairs		
Time	**Players**	**Skills**
10+	8+	*Awareness, Communication, Energy, Focus*

Running to the Centre

The group forms a circle facing inwards and taking up the maximum space that the room has to offer.

Then everyone begins to run on the spot.

At any point one of the players can initiate a movement towards the centre of the circle. As this happens, everyone joins in and runs to the centre of the circle.

Everyone stays running on the spot in this smaller circle until someone initiates the move outwards. At this point everyone runs backwards until they arrive at their initial place within the large circle.

Anyone observing the game should not be able to see who has initiated the run forwards or backwards. Don't comment on the process; simply keep repeating it until the group feels that they are communicating fully and are able to run in and out as one body. There should be a flow to the movement, rather as a wave breaks towards the shore then retreats before driving forwards again.

Time	Players	Skills
10+	8+	*Awareness, Communication, Focus*

Running in a Circle

First Version: Stopping and Starting

The group forms a big circle taking up the maximum amount of space that the room has to offer.

Everyone begins running round the room, maintaining the shape of the circle, and equidistant from the people in front and behind them.

At any point one player can initiate a sudden stop. As this happens the entire group comes to a halt. Without any verbal exchanges someone will initiate the signal to continue running again, so that, as one, the group continues running in the same direction until someone initiates a stop again.

Those watching should not be able to detect who has initiated either the break in the running or its recommencement.

Second Version: Changing the Movement

As above, the group forms a large circle and begins running around the room maintaining the distance between those in front and behind them.

At any point, just as before, any one of the players can initiate a new movement, such as a jump. Everyone then jumps up high before landing in unison back on the ground. Once they have landed, everyone crouches down in readiness for someone to initiate the move to stand. At this point the group stands together and then continues running in the circle, but this time in the opposite direction to before.

Again, observers should not be able to see who has initiated any of the stages.

Third Version: Changing Direction

As above, everyone runs round in a circle. This time, at any point a player can initiate a change of direction. Without slowing down, the group changes direction and continues to run, until there is a further initiation to run the other way.

As with all these games, an observer should not be able to see who has started the change of direction.

Note

These exercises are difficult and initially there will be much confusion. I use them regularly as warm-up games. The ability to communicate without words and to work together is strengthened with practice, but it can take time.

Players	Skills
8+	*Awareness, Communication, Focus*

Playing Tag in a Circle

The group forms a wide circle around the room, allowing for space between each player, and standing side-on to the centre of the circle so that they are facing the back of the player in front of them.

Every player thinks of a reason why they don't want to be caught, but needs to reach the person in front of them. For example:

- *'I don't want to be touched by the person behind me because they have a highly contagious disease, which is transmitted through any physical contact.'*
- *'I want to touch the person in front of me because they know the code to the main gate of the building where I live and I've lost the piece of paper I wrote it on and I don't want to be locked out for the night.'*

The group starts to run, remembering these objectives to touch and avoid touch. They must keep the size and shape of the circle the same at all times.

If someone does manage to touch the person in front of them then they must try to maintain that contact, which should be a gentle one – there is no need to grab at people or tug at their tops.

Every ten seconds or so, a designated player shouts '*Change!*', and everyone must change direction and run the other way.

Note

This game pushes everyone onto their front feet. It drives the energy forwards, but at the same time keeps everyone aware of the threat from behind. It also requires concentration to maintain the size and shape of the circle.

Time	Players	Skills
10+	8+	*Awareness, Energy, Goal-seeking, Multitasking*

Copycats

The group stands in a large circle facing inwards.

Each player selects another member of the group to observe, but it's important not to let that person know that they are watching them.

When the person being watched moves, however slightly, the person watching them must mimic that movement precisely and without exaggeration. Similarly, if they make a sound such as clearing their throat, coughing or laughing, that must be reproduced too.

The group will begin to shift quite quickly as each person copies another. It may be that ultimately the same movements are being mirrored throughout the room, but no one will know who is initiating the changes as they occur.

Time	Players	Skills
5+	8+	*Awareness, Responsiveness*

Eagle Eyes

Everyone stands in a circle with their eyes shut.

The person leading the group then asks each person a question about someone else in the group, which they must answer without looking. Once they have answered they can open their eyes, but should resist commenting on whether the answer was right or not.

The question asked will refer to something physical about another player. For example:

- *'What does John have written on his T-shirt?'*
- *'What colour nail varnish is Rachel wearing?'*
- *'What colour shoelaces does Ian have?'*

Note

You may well find it surprising how little we observe about each other in the course of everyday life. Indeed, not just of each other, but of the world around us too.

Time	Players	Skills
5+	8+	*Awareness, Focus*

Working Together

A line of players stands along one side of the room and another on the other side, facing each other.

Someone puts on some music. As the music starts, each line of players moves towards the other. They are simply walking, but allowing themselves to travel in time with the music. It is useful to start with a very slow piece that has a steady rhythm. Everyone should control their movements, keeping them informed by the style and tempo of the music, so that they are aware of how their bodies feel in the space. Both lines must reach the middle point of the room at the same time.

Once both lines are in the middle, and as the music continues, all the players must turn simultaneously and move back towards the side of the room that they started from. Everyone should reach his or her destination at the same time, before turning in unison once more and progressing towards the middle of the room. Repeat this process until all the players have developed the awareness necessary to maintain the journey to and from the centre of the room, in time with each other. The game can be practised over as many sessions as it takes to master it. Each individual player must be in control, but they must also have an acute awareness of what all the other bodies in the room are doing.

Note

As the group gets better at playing, it's fun to experiment with the music, exploring different rhythms and tempos to move to. This might mean the pace is increased, but players must still keep time with the rest of the line.

+ Music	
Time	**Skills**
30+	*Awareness, Collaboration, Control*

A Chorus of Noise

The whole group lies on the floor on their backs in a circle, with their heads facing inwards and their eyes closed.

Breathing deeply, everyone should be conscious of their breath so that the group begins to build up a rhythm with it, firstly breathing in unison, with a collective inhalation and exhalation.

When everyone is breathing comfortably together, they should gradually begin to work as individuals again. In their own time, each player should allow the exhalation of breath to become a hum, starting quietly and allowing their humming to build.

They should elongate the sound, but not try to harmonise with anyone else. The idea is not to make a beautiful noise together, nor try to copy anyone else's note.

The volume should gradually increase and everyone should open their mouths, letting the notes escape without the restriction of closed lips. When the noise level reaches a crescendo, gradually begin to decrease the volume. Slowly bring the sound back to a gentle hum before stopping altogether and simply breathing in unison, as everyone did at the start of the exercise.

Repeat the exercise, but this time as each player begins to release the sound they can do so in response to a noise created by someone else. However, anyone listening should not be able to detect who is leading with a note and who is responding. The idea is to work together in a fluid, responsive way, without manipulating the game.

Players	Skills
6+	*Awareness, Collaboration, Relaxation, Responsiveness*

Samurai

The group stands in a wide circle facing inwards so that everyone can see each other.

One person is chosen to start. They must imagine that they are some sort of fantastic Samurai warrior and do a simple movement accompanied by a corresponding noise. For example, they might kick one leg out and slice the air with the palm of their hand whilst simultaneously grunting '*Hoy!*'

The rest of the group will then repeat this movement and noise as precisely and clearly as they can. It's important that this initial action is something defined, so that it can be accurately copied.

When this prelude has been completed, the game can begin in earnest. The first player raises his or her arms above their head, joining their fingers together into a point above them.

Voicing the sound '*Ha!*', they then bring their arms down so that the fingers are pointing towards another member of the group, almost as though they are shooting the sound '*Ha!*' at that person.

In response, this second player picks up the shot, saying '*Ha!*' and lifting their arms up and connecting their fingers into a peak.

As soon as this noise has been uttered and the action completed by the second player, the people standing on either side of him or her join their fingers together and slice the air as they aim a shot at the second player's stomach. As they do so they say '*Ha!*'

Following on immediately from this, the shot returns to that second player and he or she brings their arms down so that their fingers are pointing at a third person saying '*Ha!*' as they do so.

The third player then raises their arms on the sound of '*Ha!*' and the two people either side join their hands together into a point and slice the air towards the third player, also saying '*Ha!*' The third player then shoots the '*Ha!*' to a fourth person, who will receive it in the same way. And so it goes on until a fast and consistent rhythm has been established.

The game should continue long enough for the group to play with some ease, and then add another rule. Now, if a player hesitates and by doing so breaks the rhythm, or if a player simply makes a mistake in the action or sound, then they must sit down on the spot.

Without comment, the play simply continues but with a fresh prelude. The player standing to the right of whoever has sat down imagines himself or herself a Samurai and offers an appropriate gesture and noise, which is repeated by all the others still standing. The new Samurai then becomes responsible for starting the game proper by raising their arms, forming a peak with their fingers and aiming a shot at someone so that the rhythm can build again. Now that gaps are appearing in the circle caused by people sitting down, the remaining players will have to be extra vigilant noticing the players who are positioned either side of them.

Note

This game clearly requires focus and energy. See how fast it can be played without breaking the rhythm or going wrong. The group should be working together, machine-like in its regularity and efficiency.

Time	Players	Skills
10+	10+	*Collaboration, Focus*

Passing the Stick

The group stands in a large circle facing inwards so that everyone can see each other.

Each player holds a stick in their right hand; bamboo sticks are great for this exercise.

On a given signal, everyone passes their sticks to the person on their right. As they do so, they will receive a fresh stick from the player to their left. Everyone keeps passing their sticks so that there is a continual passage around the circle, everyone passing their stick on with their right hand and receiving a new stick with their left. The flow of sticks should be uninterrupted.

When a further signal is given, everyone changes the direction of play so that now they receive the stick in their right hand and pass it on with their left.

The signal to change direction should be given frequently at irregular intervals so everyone must maintain their concentration in order to prevent the sticks from falling. If someone does drop a stick, the game is paused so that it can be retrieved, before continuing.

+ Sticks (one for each player)

Players	Skills
10+	*Awareness, Coordination, Focus*

Passing the Clap

The group stands in a large circle facing inwards so that everyone can see each other.

One player starts the game by passing a single clap to the person standing to their right. This is in turn passed on to the next person along, and so it continues around the circle. Try to maintain a steady beat.

Once this has been achieved, the player who started the game initiates things again. They now clap out a very short rhythmic phrase, which they continue to repeat.

The person to their right takes up this new rhythm, but before they pass it on, they add another simple sequence of claps to it. These first two players continue clapping the two phrases of rhythm, but the person to their right, having clapped out the first two, must then add a third, which they will continue clapping after they have passed the new sequence on. And so it moves on around the circle.

When everyone in the group is clapping and the sequence has reached the player who clapped first, then this player too must repeat the pattern of claps. This time before doing so they must change the rhythm of the first phrase of clapping that they had initially been responsible for. This is picked up by the next person, who also changes the rhythm that they had added on. So it goes on round the circle, repeating the cycle but making the rhythms and patterns increasingly more complex.

This game is challenging and can be returned to many times as players gain confidence with it.

Time	Players	Skills
10+	6+	*Awareness, Focus*

Running in Slow Motion

Everyone must line up on one side of the room and imagine that they are on the starting line for the 100-metre sprint at the Olympics.

As they stand in line, the group takes a moment or two to visualise the space, collectively deciding where the finish line is and where the tracks for each runner are. There can be as many players as can fit comfortably into the allocated space. If there are too many players to all run at once, some can act as spectators before swapping over with the runners to have a go. Any spectators must not make a noise until a winner emerges, but then they are allowed to go wild with applause!

This is a race with a difference because, although the goal is to cross the finish line before anyone else, there are certain rules that must be observed along the way:

- Everything is done in slow motion.
- Everyone starts on a given signal.
- Everyone must be looking at the imaginary finish line at all times.
- Everyone must be in motion at all times.
- Everyone must lift their feet to knee height with every step they take, and those steps must be the largest they are capable of.
- If anyone falls over, they will be immediately disqualified.

Note

On completion of the race, players may well feel exhausted since it requires a great deal of concentration to keep your balance. Every specific movement that is made needs to be controlled, so it will take a lot of energy to finish this race.

Players	Skills
2+	*Control, Coordination, Energy, Focus*

One Word at a Time

Everyone sits in a circle and one person is chosen to start the story. They do so with one word. For example, they might say '*Once*' or '*The*', or they might offer a name to get the ball rolling.

The person to their right then adds another word to the first; so if we take the above examples, they might say '*upon*' or '*boy*'. They need to follow on from the word they have just heard, responding in the moment and not anticipating or planning in advance. Next, the person to their right adds another word, as does the person to their right, and so on around the circle.

The idea is for the players to tell a coherent story using one word each at a time. You can go around the circle as many times as is needed.

This exercise is more difficult than it first appears. Initially there might be chaos. There is also a tendency for players to say more than one word at a time.

If you need to increase the group's focus, everyone can sit with their heads closer together and their eyes shut. Whispering the words might also help, but make sure everyone can hear each other.

As the group gets better at the game it can be developed further by ensuring that the story has a clear beginning, middle and end. If a clear conclusion is reached, then the players will know when to stop; however, it might be necessary for someone to conduct the story, bringing the narrative to an end when they feel it is appropriate.

Time	**Players**	**Skills**
5+	5+	*Collaboration, Focus, Responsiveness*

Word Association

Everyone stands in a circle, close to each other and facing inwards.

Somebody says the first word that comes into his or her head. The person standing to their right speaks the first word that they can think of in response to what they have just heard. The word that they choose might appear quite unrelated, but it must be the first thing that they have thought of.

The person standing next to them then says the first word that comes to their mind, and so on round the circle. You can keep going round as many times as it feels useful to do so. If there is hesitation, or laughter, or comment of any kind, then stop and start again.

Note

The game encourages the players to listen to each other. However, each word can only arise as a result of the one immediately before it and not due to an association with something mentioned a few turns earlier. Players shouldn't take time to think before they speak. They mustn't censor the word that comes to mind first. The pace of the game should be quick and the rhythm consistent.

Time	Players	Skills
5+	5+	*Focus, Responsiveness*

Unlocking the Senses

One person is chosen to stand in front of the rest of the group, who line up across the other side of the room. The individual player holds their hand out in front of them, palm facing out.

One by one, the other players cross the room and places their own palm against the player's outstretched hand. The single player should observe closely how the others move. Listen to the rhythm and pace of their walks. Notice any sound generated by the movement of their clothes. Are they taller or shorter, and what physical impact, if any, does this have? Do they have a particular smell? Does their body give off heat? The single player should make sure they have got a really good sense of each person, before telling them that they can withdraw their palm and sit down.

Repeat the process – but this time the single player is blindfolded as each player comes up to touch their hand. The order in which people cross the room should be changed at each stage of the exercise.

As each person touches the outstretched hand, the single player must say the name of the person they think it is out loud without removing the blindfold. They won't be told if they are right or wrong, so they can say names more than once if they change their mind. Continue until everyone has made contact again, then the player may remove the blindfold and discover how many people they named correctly.

Repeat the process – but this time no one will actually touch the hand. They will leave a centimeter or so between the two palms. Again, the single player must see how many names they can correctly guess.

+ A blindfold

Time	Players	Skills
20+	5+	*Awareness, Collaboration, Responsiveness*

Engaging All the Senses

In order to play this game, a facilitator must prepare and bring in a series of objects:

- Paper cups, one for each player, inside of which is a small amount of a substance or liquid that has a strong smell. (These are best prepared the night before to maximise the intensity of the smell.) Each player's cup should carry a different scent: for example, a dollop of suncream, a spray of perfume, a few drops of vinegar, or some grass.
- A collection of objects that are not sharp, but that have interesting and varying textures. For example, a piece of driftwood, a smooth pebble, a cold metal spoon, a feather. Again, there should be as many objects as there are players.
- A selection of music, six or seven pieces, with different rhythms and tempos, and belonging to different genres – and something to play the music on.
- Avoiding nuts and other foods which potentially provoke allergies, small pieces of food on the end of cocktail sticks, enough for each player to have their own. The same food item can be used for each player. Tangerine segments work really well. The facilitator should check for allergies before starting the game.
- A number of pictures ranging in their subject matter: a rolling landscape, a black-and-white photo of a couple on their wedding day, an abstract painting, a portrait, etc. Again, each player will have their own.

Everyone sits in a circle wearing a blindfold. Since they will be sitting in this imposed darkness for some time, every player should make sure that they are warm and comfortable. They should also understand that this environment is a safe one, where no tricks will be played on them.

The facilitator will place an object on the floor just in front of each player, who obviously won't be able to see what it is. When instructed to do so, the player picks up their object and spends some time touching it and playing with it, feeling its texture and contours. There is no need to work out what the object actually is – and some shapes will be more obvious than others anyway. Players should allow themselves to respond freely to the sensations, memories and associations that are provoked by their contact with this thing. They should remain silent unless the facilitator asks them to share their experience out loud with the rest of the group. The facilitator may ask a number of people to describe their responses, before inviting everyone to pass their object on to the person on their right. Now everyone will have a new object to explore, and the facilitator may ask different people for their experiences. The exercise continues until everyone has touched a number of different objects.

The facilitator clears the objects away whilst everyone sits with their blindfolds on. When the space is clear, a cup will be placed in front of each of them. They will be asked to pick it up and smell the contents. Again, there is no need to be literal in naming the scent. Players should allow themselves to picture what it evokes in them. Does the smell bring back a place they have visited? Perhaps it reminds them of a person, or a time in their lives? It may simply provoke emotions that have little to do with anything they have experienced concretely. As with the objects, the facilitator will ask some of the group to share their reactions before asking them to pass the cup to their right, so that everyone has a new smell to experience. Each player should have a chance to experience at least three different aromas.

The facilitator will then clear the cups away, as the group sits blindfolded. Having checked for food allergies, they will then place a cocktail stick in each player's hand, but they should not put it in their mouths until they are told to do so. Everyone must have the experience simultaneously. It may take some time for the signal to eat to be given, but that anticipation is part of the experience. When everyone has eaten, the facilitator may ask for some reactions before clearing the cocktail sticks away.

Now the group will be asked to lie on the floor on their backs, still wearing the blindfolds. The facilitator will play some music. After each track, or part of a track, some of the players may be asked to comment on their reactions before the music is changed. Everyone should experience five or six different passages of music.

Finally, everyone is asked to take off their blindfolds, which may feel a little shocking at first as eyes adjust to the light. Each player is given an image to look at. They should study the picture and notice what feelings it provokes. Again, some of them will be asked to describe their sensations before they pass the picture on and receive another. This will continue until everyone has considered three or four different images.

Note

This is a very intense exercise, which may provoke surprising responses in the players. It may well be that everyone reacts more strongly to certain things than others. They may have a sensation, which once they know what it was that they were smelling, touching, tasting or listening to, seems incongruous. The important thing is that everyone becomes aware of how potent our senses are when used fully. We simply need to engage our senses immersively in a way that need not be rational, in order to use them as triggers, unlocking us emotionally and imaginatively. Notice how anticipation plays a part here, and that anticipation is almost as tangible as the thing itself.

+ Blindfolds; assorted objects, liquids, foods, music and images

Time	Players	Skills
30+	5+	*Analysis, Communication, Responsiveness*

Virtual Gallery

In preparation for this game all the players should go to an art gallery and walk around independently of each other. If you can't get to an exhibition, then look through books of paintings.

Each player chooses one of the pictures and studies it in detail. They must notice as much as they can about it – for instance, the brushstrokes, colour, atmosphere, the physicality of the painting, the emotions and thoughts it provokes, the story it tells, etc. They can choose landscape or portrait, abstract or realistic – but must opt for a picture that they are drawn to. They should make sure that they can visualise it when they turn their back to it.

When the group reconvenes, they are going to create a virtual gallery held within everyone's imaginations. Each member will describe their painting for the others, referring to it as though it is hanging on the wall for everyone to see. The details must be recalled with accuracy: the subject matter, the colours, the light, the brushstrokes, the atmosphere created by the artist, etc. Those listening should get a sense of each painting, without having physically seen it themselves – and can ask questions about the artwork if they require further information.

Note

This game helps each player to gauge how well they can recreate the image of something when it is no longer present. For those listening, it will encourage them to respond and connect imaginatively, despite the physical absence of the thing described.

+ Books of paintings

Time	Players	Skills
10+	5+	*Awareness, Communication, Imagination*

Laughing and Crying

Everyone lays in a circle on their backs with their heads facing towards the centre of the circle.

As they lay there, everyone should smile. They must allow themselves to feel that smile spread across their face, enjoying the sensation of smiling.

Now, everyone should repeat the sound '*Ha-ha-ha*' continuously.

Observe the results.

Now, in exactly the same position, everyone alters their breath and rhythm, so that the noise that their make sounds like a continual pattern of sobs.

They should notice how they feel.

Note

This is a very basic way of using breath and rhythm to provoke emotion. When we embody the sound physically it is extraordinary what responses we can experience emotionally.

Players	Skills
5+	*Analysis, Physicality, Responsiveness*

Overcoming Inhibitions

The facilitator gives every player a piece of paper with the name of an animal written on it. Players should only get to see the name of the animal that they have been given. Unbeknownst to the group, someone else in the room will have a piece of paper with the same animal written on it.

Players should not use noise, but play physically with becoming the animals in the space. They can do this by working quite literally: for example, forming an elephant's trunk with an arm, going on all fours and stretching like a cat. Or they might explore in a more abstract way, expressing their animal in a manner that conjures the creature for them, but may not be immediately recognisable to anyone watching.

Everyone plays around in the space, exploring different elements of their animal without inhibition, until the facilitator says to go and find a mate of the same species! During the search for companionship, in order to establish whether they have found the appropriate partner, players are permitted to make a noise. So, for a cat a '*meow*' would be sufficient, and a player may need to howl if they are a wolf. Everyone keeps searching until they meet the same animal as them; once pairs have been matched up, they can interact together.

Note

Sometimes games like this, that seem the most ridiculous to begin with, can serve to liberate actors. They give the permission to play freely, and although they may seem silly, they have a purpose. Here, for example, players must really work without inhibition, and responsively within the group.

+ Pre-prepared cards		
Time	**Players**	**Skills**
20+	10+	*Physicality, Responsiveness*

The Letter

Everyone forms a wide circle, sitting on the floor, so that there is enough space for players to see each other easily.

The facilitator hands one player an envelope with a blank sheet of paper inside it. They tell the player that there is nothing on the page, but that they must react to whatever news is written there; since the page is blank they must invent the content. There should be no planning ahead for this. The player mustn't map out what they are going to do. They simply open the envelope and let the ideas that come unfold in that moment.

The player should not make a statement revealing what is in the letter. For example, they shouldn't look at it and then shout, '*Yippee I have inherited a million pounds from my old Auntie Doris!*' Instead, they must allow the information they imagine to be there to resonate with them – and then react to it without resorting to a literal sharing of information. They must imagine that whatever the news is, good or bad, it is a surprise to them.

Once the first player has responded to their imaginary news, they fold the paper back into the envelope and pass it to another player in the circle, not necessarily either of those sitting next to them.

When the next person receives the envelope, they should take a moment or two to refocus before opening it and reacting to its surprising contents. Everyone should resist planning a response before opening the envelope. They should simply observe the behaviour of the person who currently holds it without thinking about what they are going to do when they get the letter. The envelope is passed on until each player has had a turn.

Note

This is a difficult game because it is very tempting for each player to plan what they will do before the envelope reaches them, and the exercise requires them not to do that. They must take their time to imagine the news, and let it work on them without imposing any emotion on it. The game requires actors to *do* and not to show. They must, therefore, really engage in the task of reading the information rather than jumping straight to a presentation of how they assume they might feel.

+ Blank paper in an envelope	
Players	**Skills**
20+	*Imagination, Physicality, Responsiveness*

PART TWO

CHARACTER

Part Two concentrates on character, with all of the games and exercises aiming to help the actor begin the process of transformation that leads to the creation of a role. This is not without its complications. When we reflect on our own lives, it is apparent that our behaviour is not always consistent; we may exhibit contradictory characteristics dependent on the circumstances that we find ourselves in. Character cannot be an immutable and fixed entity. As actors, in order to spark life into a role, we must look for the contradictions and inconsistencies that live within all human beings.

This chapter features some straightforward games, other exercises require close consideration of the text that you are working on. Some require preparation, others ask you to work spontaneously. The games can be played if you are working on a play – but are also useful workshop exercises in their own right for the creation and development of a character. Generally the exercises require a facilitator – a teacher, workshop leader or director – to implement them, but if you are an actor working on your own to develop your character you can draw from the essence of each and apply the ideas to your private preparation.

In order to encourage this sort of solo exploration – but also to offer a script of sorts for the facilitator – I have addressed many of the exercises directly to the actor. Most of the exercises will take varying lengths of time, depending on the size of the group, and whether you are working individually or collectively. Where appropriate I have noted the exercises that require the actor to prepare in advance.

Physical Essences

This game can be played using different categories. I have chosen to use motor vehicles, but I have included further ideas at the end that you might like to try as well. You can come up with many more versions. Remember the game should not be taken literally. I am not asking actors to *become* a car, but rather to explore the essence of their imaginative connection to it. There should be no words spoken until the end; this is a game that asks actors to explore qualities physically.

Everyone stands in a circle facing inwards with their eyes shut. The facilitator will go around the circle tapping each actor on the shoulder. Actors who are tapped three times must imagine that they possess the qualities associated with a Mercedes Benz, two taps for a Mini Cooper, and one tap for a Volkswagen camper van.

When told to do so, everyone opens their eyes and moves around the room, thinking about the qualities associated with the vehicle and internalising them so that they take a human form. The movements should be affected by this internal connection; the rhythm and tempo should shift. As actors engage with each other in the space, they should not speak, but pay attention to how they relate to those around them. How much space do they occupy? Who has right of way if they get bunched together? How do they feel in each other's company? They should take their time to explore physical qualities, but resist any urge to demonstrate them, so they can be quite subtle in their movements. The idea is to embody the *essence* of each car, and find its physical expression from an internal starting point.

Once the interactions between actors have been established and everyone has had enough time to explore the space, the facilitator will ask each player to find those people who they believe are in the same category of vehicle as them. So all the Mercedes will form a group, as will the Minis and the camper vans. Once groups are standing where they think they belong, they can find out from each other if they have made the right choice, and why they thought that they should be with that group of people.

Ideas for Further Categories

- Explore the qualities that you associate with a type of music: opera, rock, country…
- Explore the qualities that you associate with acting in: a Greek Tragedy, a play by Anton Chekhov, a soap opera…

Skills

Character, Imagination, Inner life, Physicality, Rhythm, Status

Animals

You can use this exercise in a general way when considering your character, or you can apply it to a particular scene or section of text. Thinking about animals in relation to your character is useful, and there are many ways of going about it. Here is a starting point from which you can develop your ideas. You may need to research a particular animal in order to engage with the exercise fully.

Consider which animal you most associate with your character. There may be more than one, and your ideas might shift as your work on the script progresses. However, you can only really work with one animal at a time.

These questions might help you:

- *If my character were an animal, where would it be in the food chain?*
- *If my character were an animal, what would its natural habitat be?*
- *What is my character's habitual rhythm and tempo, and what animal best represents this?*

Consider these three questions and choose an animal on the basis of your answers. Here is an example, imagining that I am playing Lady Macbeth:

- *If my character were an animal, where would it be in the food chain?*
  I know that my character runs a household and so she has some power. I also know that she achieves her goal by persuading her husband to kill the king, but she doesn't physically commit the act herself.
- *If my character were an animal, what would its natural habitat be?*
  I know that Lady Macbeth is comfortable in her household. She holds sway over her servants. She is hostess to some of the most powerful players in the land. She is not afraid to be visible as she goes about her business. However, I also know that the king is killed under the cover of darkness, and that she uses stealth and subterfuge to get her way.

- *What is my character's habitual rhythm and tempo, and what animal best represents this?* Lady Macbeth initially seems quite a smooth operator. She appears gracious with the king as she welcomes him into her home and she manages her guests with ease. She also has to be watchful and increasingly wary in order to get away with her crime. She has bursts of energy as she engages with her husband. She pounces with deadly intent when the time calls for it.

Having looked at my answers, the animal I would choose is a lynx. These creatures are fairly high up the food chain, although they are not capable of bringing down an animal much bigger than themselves. To do this they would need to hunt in a pack, and although they are generally solitary predators, they do stalk their food in small groups when the occasion requires. They would have to be wary of animals bigger and stronger than themselves. Their natural habitat is in high-altitude forests with dense vegetation. They wait in long grasses; they can also climb trees and swim. They strike from hidden places. The lynx moves with grace and fluidity, with the easy movements typical of a cat. However, they can pick up speed and when they pounce it is with sudden and deadly intensity. Their rhythm and tempo can be unpredictable.

Using Lady Macbeth as an example is simply a way of clarifying the process for you, but your own answers might be quite different to mine.

The more time you have spent observing the animal you have chosen prior to the start of the exercise, the better; though you can begin with broad brushstrokes, which can then be refined through repetition of the exercise. At first you may lack physical precision, but you will still learn a great deal about your character and how they interact with others.

If you are working generally on your character, set up a context within which to improvise. This might be a situation mentioned in the play itself, something that happens to your character offstage; or you could choose to construct an environment that is not referred to in the text at all, but which will provide insight into the behaviour of your character. For example, you might want to improvise around a family gathering, a job interview, a wedding or a funeral, etc. Identify the given circumstances: time, place, weather, where you have just come from, what you want, and so on.

If you are using specific text then obviously that will dictate your setting. You can then either improvise the scene using your own words or use the dialogue as written.

Engage with the improvisation or dialogue exploring your character's behaviour through that of the animal you have chosen. To begin with, work with a heightened physicality. For example, if you have chosen an animal that is very low down in the food chain, your responses to the other characters would mirror that. You might be frightened to expose yourself to danger. You might keep your distance from those around you, always retreating when they approach. If you have chosen an animal that views the world from a high vantage point – a bird of prey perhaps – then you might try to be physically higher than those around you. You might play the scene or improvisation standing on tiptoe, on chairs, or on tables, as you to try to get a sense of looking down on those around you. If you have chosen an animal that is very languid and slow-paced – a sloth, for example – you would explore this in the way that you move. You might lie down for parts of the scene, or settle in chairs for as long as possible. The way you pick up objects or go about your activities might be measured and even and languorous.

Remember that everyone else involved in the scene or improvisation will also behave in a way that incorporates the qualities of the animal that they have chosen, and you will have to be responsive to that. You may want to curl up and rest, but the predator next to you may not allow you to feel comfortable doing that. You may also encounter someone who has chosen a similar animal to you, so you will have to negotiate any rivalry or conflicts that arise from this. You are not playing the animal itself, you are still a human being, but you are embodying certain qualities of that animal in the exploration of your character.

You should repeat the exercise, refining your choices each time, so that finally the qualities live in you, but are not necessarily outwardly displayed. For example, your chosen animal might naturally be drawn to dark corners and underground burrows, but the script dictates that your character is in the centre of a dance floor, fully visible to those around him. The desire to hide, as explored through the animal, will fuel the inner life of the character, creating conflicting rhythms in you and informing your responses to everything that surrounds you, both in terms of the physical world and the people that populate it.

+ Preparation

Skills

Awareness, Character, Imagination, Physicality, Rhythm

A Variation on Hot-seating

This exercise asks you to examine what is kept *hidden* by your character, and what they *choose to reveal*, in a more specific way.

In order to establish an environment where it is plausible that your character would reveal intimate aspects of their life more readily, imagine that they are talking to a therapist. Another actor from the group will take the role of the therapist. Two chairs should be positioned so that they face each other but are at a comfortable distance apart. The 'therapist' will sit in one and you will sit in the other in character. For the purposes of this exercise anyone else watching will remain silent; it is as if they are not in the room.

The therapist will then proceed to ask the following questions and you will answer them as though you are your character in a therapy session. When the questions refer to other people you should refer to other characters in the play. Both you and the therapist will need to have done research so that you understand the context of the play in terms of its historical and geographical location; this will inform both the questions and the answers.

- *How would you describe yourself?*
  Think of this in terms of your physicality, your character traits, the moral choices you make, and your behaviour throughout the course of the play.
- *How do you think other people view you?*
- *How do you like to present yourself?*
  What is it that you want other people to see when they meet you and spend time with you?
- *What information about yourself do you like to keep hidden?*
  What thoughts and actions would you not wish to be revealed to anyone else?
- *Is there a part of your life that you consider unlived?*
  Are there things that you have not yet done in your life that you would like to do?

- *What would enable you to bring those unlived parts of you to life? What would need to change in order for that to happen?*

When these questions have been fully examined and explored, the therapist will bring the session to an end, and the rest of the group can then discuss anything that they noticed while watching.

If you are an actor working on your own, then you can answer each of these questions during your personal preparation time.

+ Preparation
Skills
Analysis, Character, Imagination, Inner life

Speed Dating

To prepare for this exercise you should have undertaken a close reading of the play. It is also a worthwhile exercise if you are not working on a play – but are inventing your own character.

Ask yourself as many questions that are relevant from the list below:

- *What is your full name?*
- *How old are you?*
- *Have you any brothers or sisters?*
- *Where were you born?*
- *Where did you grow up?*
- *Where do you live now?*
- *What was school like for you?*
- *Who was your best friend at school?*
- *What did you want to be when you grew up?*
- *What is your job now?*
- *Do you like your job?*
- *Are you gay or straight?*
- *Are you in a relationship?*
- *Are you happy in that relationship?*
- *What is the worst thing you have ever done?*
- *What is the thing that you are proudest of?*
- *Who do you love the most in the world?*
- *What is your greatest fear?*
- *Do you vote? If so, who do you vote for?*
- *What music do you listen to?*
- *What is your favourite book?*
- *What is your favourite film?*
- *What is your idea of a perfect day?*
- *Do you smoke?*
- *Do you take drugs?*
- *Do you drink alcohol?*
- *What is your favourite drink?*

- *Who do you hate most in the world?*
- *When or where were you the happiest in your life?*
- *What is your favourite item of clothing?*
- *Do you do any sport?*
- *Do you have any hobbies?*
- *What makes you angry?*
- *If you could change one thing about yourself, what would it be?*
- *What secret about yourself would you least want anyone to know?*
- *Have you ever thought about suicide?*
- *Do you drive? If so, what do you drive?*
- *Do you watch the news?*
- *Do you read any newspapers or magazines?*
- *What turns you on?*
- *What is the landscape you are most comfortable in?*
- *What is your favourite season?*
- *What is your favourite colour?*
- *Do you have any health problems?*
- *What do you think about the monarchy?*
- *Who is your hero or heroine?*
- *Have you ever committed a crime?*
- *What was your first love?*
- *If you were an animal, what would you be?*
- *If you were an element, what would you be: earth, water, air or fire?*

Having answered these questions to the best of your ability and in relation to the nature of the text you are working on, you are now ready to go speed dating! Bring to the rehearsal or workshop any possessions that you think your character might carry and wear clothes that you feel are appropriate; think about really specific things, like the height of their shoes, how many buttons are done up on their shirt, whether they wear a jacket, whether their garments are flowing or restrictive, etc.

Imagine that your character has arrived at a speed-dating event. You are here to meet someone. You may be looking for romance or just friendship; you can decide this at the outset but your decision may alter depending on who you are talking to.

The chairs will be set out in two concentric circles, one inside the other. You can sit where you like so that each of you is facing another character.

When the facilitator says '*Go!*' you should start a conversation with the person sitting opposite you. The aim is to try to get to know them to see whether you might be suited either romantically or as friends. The conversation could start with a banal comment about the weather, but as it continues the questions listed above will arise, depending on what you want to know from the other person, and how you choose to reveal yourself in the answers. The facilitator can introduce topics of discussion, linked to the themes of the play. Listen to these instructions, but behave as though the facilitator is not present. After two minutes the facilitator will say '*Change*' and the outer circle of people will move round one space to their right. Everyone will now be facing a new person and can start up a two-minute conversation with them.

You can play the game for as long as it keeps throwing up new ideas, discoveries, conversations and relationships. Like a true speed-dating event, at the end of the session you can rate and rank other prospective suitors.

+ Preparation

Skills

Awareness, Character, Imagination, Responsiveness, Status

Observation

Consider your character in terms of the following:

- Characteristics (vain, insecure, wild, etc.)
- Rhythm and tempo (inner and outer)
- Mannerisms
- Tics
- Idiosyncrasies
- Patterns of speech
- Dress style
- Status

Having gone through this list, find someone that reminds you of your character. This could be a stranger, or someone already known to you. You should avoid anyone that you know too intimately as your close involvement with them might inhibit your freedom to play.

Observe this person as closely as you can. Obviously this will require discretion on your part!

Create a biography for them: their name, job, history of relationships, etc. You will need to use your imagination to fill the gaps in your concrete knowledge of them. You can refer to the fifty questions listed in the previous *Speed Dating* exercise, in order to create a detailed profile.

During the exercise, dress as the person you have observed and bring in any belongings that you think they might carry, such as a handbag, book, newspaper, packed lunch, etc.

You are going to engage in at least two hours of improvisation as the person you have observed, during which time you can interact with the other people present as and when you feel it is appropriate to do so. The context of the improvisation is that everyone is here for an audition for an amateur-theatre production, although due to terrible traffic the director of the play you are auditioning for has been delayed and everyone is waiting. Be specific with the given circumstances in terms of time and place, etc. You can decide as a group the title of the play – real or invented – in which everyone present wants to be given a role.

You must justify why the person you have observed wants to be part of the show: perhaps they are lonely or have aspirations that go beyond their day job. They might want to sleep with the director! Be specific and refer to the biography you have created to help you flesh out these choices.

The facilitator might offer further information for you to play with during the improvisation. For example, maybe one person might hate another, or they are desperate for a drink, or they have another appointment that they need to get to. Whatever instructions are given, incorporate them into your exploration without acknowledging the presence of the facilitator. You will be improvising for a considerable length of time, which will allow you to absorb the qualities of the person you have observed, so that you can begin to embody them without forcing anything.

Note

This exercise allows all of the actors to engage with elements of the characters that they are playing, but within a different context to the play that they are working on. In doing so, it serves to provide a liberating examination of behaviour that can lead to a deeper understanding of each character's needs, habits, rhythms, characteristics and methods of interaction, when returning to the actual text.

+ Preparation

Skills

Awareness, Character, Physicality, Rhythm, Status

Solitude

Think of an activity that your character might do when they are alone. Choose something that is referred or alluded to during the course of the play, but that the audience doesn't actually witness as part of the onstage action. For example, your character might mention that they love to paint in their spare time, although there isn't actually a scene where we see them doing it.

Assemble any objects that you need in order to engage in your task. Nothing should be mimed. Set up the space you are working in to represent, as far as possible, the room in which your activity takes place. So if you are writing a love letter, apart from the paper and pen required, you might like to bring in a lamp. You might bring in a rug for the floor, some books to stack around you, a glass and a bottle of wine, a photograph of your partner; anything that that will help you to create the atmosphere of the setting. If you know, because it is evident from the script, that your character is chaotic, you might bring in papers to scatter over the floor, a half-eaten sandwich, some clothes discarded wherever you took them off.

When everything is set up, engage in your task for a minimum of five minutes and for no longer than ten. The idea is for you to explore your character as they are in private, which may well be different from their public persona. You must at no point think of this as a performance, despite the fact that you are being watched by the rest of the group. Engage fully with the task and allow yourself to experience your character's solitude.

You may or may not make noise during the exercise. Your character might talk to themselves, or sing along to music, or clear their throat frequently. Or they may, just as reasonably, stay silent.

+ Preparation; props (optional)

Skills

Analysis, Character, Focus, Inner life, Physicality

Characteristics

After a close reading of the play make a list of the characteristics or personality traits that you believe your character possesses. Having done this, choose the three that intrigue you the most, and that you feel are the most prevalent in your character's behaviour. These can be traits shown or kept concealed during the play.

Examples of characteristics:

- Aggressive
- Vain
- Maternal
- Vindictive
- Childlike
- Sensual
- Timid

Having chosen three characteristics to explore, create a situation for your character. As with the previous exercise, use the text itself to stimulate your imagination. For example, if in the course of the play your character refers to the fact that they paint in their spare time, then you might choose to explore that activity during this exercise. In order to engage with the situation that you have chosen, you will need to pay detailed attention to the given circumstances that surround it. Ask yourself what your character's objective is – in other words, what does your character need? Be specific about time and place and what your character has been doing previously.

Think of three tasks your character must undertake in order to achieve their need in this context.

Set up the scene, locating it in a specific place and bring in any props that are required. Avoid sharp objects such as knives and razors.

This exercise asks you to engage with your tasks whilst exploring the characteristics that you have identified, both physically and psychologically. Each task should take five minutes to complete, and should reflect one of your characteristics. In the course of your exploration these characteristics might overlap, but each should be clearly defined. In order to do this you will need to rehearse the exercise prior to the session, so this is not simply an improvisation. However, as you explore, you should discover new things and not be straitjacketed by your preparation. Work to heighten each characteristic; this is about playing with extremes. It is about full embodiment, not subtle suggestion.

After fifteen minutes the exercise ends. You may have completed what you set out to do or you may still be in the process of it, but each characteristic should have been explored.

Here is an example:

Facts taken from the script itself:

- I am besotted with my partner.
- I find out that they have been unfaithful to me.
- I confront my partner and they humiliate me.
- I ultimately go on to murder my partner.
- I refer to the fact that I paint in order to release tension.

Characteristics taken from my onstage behaviour:

- Insecure
- Vain
- Jealous
- Passionate
- Loving
- Possessive
- Creative
- Generous
- Wild
- Vindictive

The three characteristics that I am going to focus on:

- Loving
- Wild
- Vindictive

The given circumstances of my imaginary situation:

- It is two in the morning.
- It is still very hot; the air has not quite cooled from the previous day and is warming for the next one.
- I am in my studio.
- I have just found out that my lover has been unfaithful to me with someone they met at work.
- I can't sleep and I need to release my tension through painting.
- I am plagued with images of my lover in bed with someone else.
- I am going to paint a picture of my lover as I would like to think of them, so that I can stop these disturbing mental pictures.

Tasks:

- I go through a box of photographs to find a picture of my partner that reflects happier times.
- I clean my paintbrushes, set up my paint and get the paper/canvas ready.
- I paint a picture of the photograph.

Exploring the characteristics:

- My *loving* feelings will be explored through the way I examine each photograph; how I touch the pictures, how I lay each one out for selection. Each photograph holds a memory of our relationship and that will be reflected in my physical response to them.
- The way I clean my paintbrushes and set up my materials will allow me to express my *vindictive* nature. I want to punish my lover for the way they have treated me. My thoughts are of revenge and I play through scenarios in my head where they are humiliated, begging for a forgiveness that I won't give. This will be reflected in the physical way I go about my task.
- I begin to paint and, as I do so, any precision is lost. I work with abandon, using sweeping

brushstrokes, slapping on colour, not caring if the paint goes on the paper or on me. My physicality mirrors my *wildness*.

During the course of the exercise you may find that previous characteristics reintroduce themselves. For instance, within this context, I might feel a pang of love for my partner as I clean the brushes. As I paint with abandon I might be overwhelmed by vindictiveness again. You shouldn't isolate each characteristic, exploring them separately in a manner that can seem schizophrenic. The characteristics can ebb and flow, but each must be explored physically and find full expression.

+ Preparation; props (optional)

Skills

Analysis, Character, Physicality, Responsiveness

The Other Side of the Coin

Make a list of some characteristics that, on a close reading of the play, you think your character possesses. Choose three of them to explore for the purpose of this exercise.

For example, if I am playing Othello, I might choose to explore the following characteristics:

- Noble
- High status
- Romantic

Now consider alternative characteristics to the ones you have chosen. For example:

- Base
- Insecure
- Possessive

Combine your lists and from all six characteristics choose three to explore. Select three that work in opposition to each other. For example, I might now choose to play with the following:

- High status
- Romantic
- Insecure

Play the scene that you are working on, but allow your point of concentration to focus on only one of these characteristics at a time. Begin with the first on your list. When the facilitator claps their hands, switch to explore the second quality, and when you hear the facilitator clap again, switch to the third. Each time the facilitator claps you must explore a different characteristic from your list, shifting between the three throughout the scene. Only one actor at a time will explore their characteristics in this way through the scene. However, as the behaviour of one character changes, inevitably all the other actors involved will be affected by the shifts, and will need to work responsively.

For example, I begin working with the idea that Othello is very high status. This informs my relationships with those around me, how I move, how I view the world. The facilitator claps, and I now focus on my love for my wife in the play. Everything I say and do is now influenced by my thoughts of her and the love I feel when I think of her. The facilitator claps again, and I begin to explore my feelings of insecurity. I allow the thought to drop in that perhaps my wife is not in love with me after all, perhaps those around me are untrustworthy, perhaps I am not as respected in society as I had thought I was. The facilitator claps again, and I view those around me as being lower in status again. Another clap, and I remember my love once more, allowing the warm feelings to flood in.

Continue until you have explored the scene through the lens of your opposing characteristics. During the exercise embody them fully so that when you come to rehearse the scene later you can allow them to be less outwardly visible, having really explored them so that you understand the contradictions without feeling the need to display them.

This exercise allows you to explore the opposing characteristics that exist within all human beings, allowing you to work at a deeper, more textured level. There should always be an alternative path that your character could have taken, despite the fact that the text dictates the choices that they ultimately do make. By looking for contradictory qualities, you bring a character to life, highlighting the potential for your character to travel alternative pathways in their story. This is not only illuminating for you as an actor, but also keeps the choices you make unpredictable for an audience.

+ Preparation

Skills

Analysis, Character, Inner life

Inner and Outer Tempo-Rhythms

This exercise can follow the previous two, or stand alone as a means of exploring the contradictory tempo-rhythms inherent within a character. Often, how someone presents themself will not mirror how they are actually feeling. They can appear outwardly calm, for instance, whilst inside their heart is beating wildly. It is useful to use a metronome for this exercise, though a facilitator can also tap out the beat. A whole company can work simultaneously, all engaging with the same tempo at once, or you can watch each other exploring different tempos, depending on your time frame and needs. Or you can try the exercise in your own preparation time.

Engage in a simple physical task. This can be as basic as tying your shoelaces, or you might engage in an activity referred to in the script, or one that is part of the onstage action, as you did in the previous exercise.

Consider the outer tempo-rhythm that your character displays during their task. For instance, if you are washing up the dishes, your character might wash them in a systematic, orderly fashion, slowly gliding the cloth over each plate, before laying it down carefully to dry. In this case, set the metronome to a steady measured beat (or if you are working without a metronome, then the facilitator can tap out a regular beat).

Engage with the task, allowing your rhythm and tempo to be guided by the beat that has been established.

If your task is accomplished quickly then simply repeat it until you have had a chance to really embody the beat. Let it inform how you engage with your activity.

Once the tempo has been established and embodied then alter the pace of the beat. This should reflect the possible *inner* life of your character at that moment. Perhaps your character is in love and the object of their desire is due to arrive imminently. Perhaps they are planning to murder their dinner guests! Perhaps they are nervous about an important speech that they are due to give that evening. The given circumstances dictated by the text will inform your choices here.

Perform the same task, but this time do so in accordance with the new tempo that has been set. Your movement may now be more erratic, the pace swifter, the body more agitated.

When you have explored the task in the light of this altered beat, decide which of these tempos should be heard in the room. Perhaps you will choose the outer tempo-rhythm to be tapped out by the metronome or facilitator.

Engage with your task once more, but this time, although you will be influenced by the beat that you can hear, allow the physical memory of the opposing tempo to be present in you. So, for example, although you may wash those dishes in a measured way, you will retain the memory of the inner agitation that you previously experienced. You can allow the inner motor to find expression through the steady outer tempo.

You can play around with the beat. You can listen to the inner pulse as opposed to the outer. You can obviously experiment with different tempos from those I have outlined. The aim is to explore the contradictory forces within a character, according to the given circumstances and through the physical embodiment of opposing tempos. Consider the feelings that are generated in you as a result of playing with different tempos and rhythms, and how these relate to your character.

+ A metronome, if possible

Skills

Character, Inner life, Physicality, Rhythm

Endowment of Objects

Think of an object that your character might need to find in a hurry under certain circumstances. For example, keys, a credit card, a passport, a driving licence, a needle and thread, or a particular book. Imagine a scenario in which your character needs that object urgently but has lost it. Your character only has five minutes to find it.

Here are some examples:

- Your character is just about to go to a job interview. She has to leave in five minutes, but the button on the only appropriate shirt she owns has just fallen off. She needs to find a needle and thread to sew it back on. The shirt is unwearable without the button on it.
- Your character needs to get to the hospital immediately as his wife is giving birth to their first child. He has to find his car keys or he won't be able to get there on time.
- Your character has an exam that she must leave for in five minutes in order to make it on time. She knows that a specific question will be asked in the exam paper, but her mind has gone blank and she can't remember the answer. It is contained in a specific book, which she cannot put her hands on.

You should choose objects and situations that are relevant to the text you are working on.

Endow your chosen object with the need that it represents for your character, other than the most immediate and material one. So, for instance, if we consider the list of objects that I have given you as examples, here is a possible greater need that the character might associate with each one.

- *Object* – a needle and thread
  Need – my character has always felt that she is chaotic and not fully capable of organising her life. She *needs* to be in control. The needle and thread represent that control.

- *Object* – my car keys
  Need – my character has cheated on his wife with another woman. He has been wracked with guilt ever since. He must get to the hospital in time because he *needs* to feel like a good husband. The car keys represent his ability to do that.
- *Object* – a book
  Need – my character has continually felt stupid throughout her life. Her parents have always told her that she is not as clever as her brother. At school she has always struggled to keep up. She *needs* respect. The book represents the means to gain this respect.

The facilitator will hide the object prior to the start of the hunt. Each actor enters the room, watched by the rest of the group. They will have five minutes to search for their missing object, having endowed it with a greater sense of what it represents to their character.

Through the use of endowment, the actor is able to gain a deeper sense of their character's needs and just how pressing they are. It also helps with work on personalisation, enabling the actor to be really specific about the objects that their character possesses and refers to.

+ Preparation; appropriate objects

Skills

Character, Inner life, Physicality

Visualisation

Before you begin this exercise it is important for you to be as relaxed as possible in order to be as open and receptive to images as possible. To that end I have included a relaxation exercise to begin with. You can develop this as required.

Lie on the floor on your back with your legs stretched out in front of you and your arms by your sides. Begin by noticing your breathing. There is no need to do anything about it, simply acknowledge that air flows in and out of you regularly. Put your hand on your diaphragm if it helps you to connect with the deep and steady flow of your breath.

Now isolate each part of your body and mentally give it permission to relax. As you consciously relax your toes, feet, calves, thighs and so on, feel the weight of the floor beneath you. Your body can afford to let go of tension, knowing that it is supported by the floor at all times. As you lie there you should be increasingly aware of your breath deepening and your body becoming heavier as each part of it relaxes into the floor.

Begin to allow images related to your character to float into your consciousness. Do not censor these images: they could be of anything and associated with any moment that your character experiences. Your mind might fill with a particular colour; you might see the hem of a dress; you might catch a glimpse of a wedding ring glinting on a hand; you might see a picture of a particular landscape that your character is walking through. The images can be poetic or mundane. You might visualise a pint glass, half-empty on a tartan beer mat; a plate of chips; washing hung out to dry as rain clouds gather. Allow your mind to swirl around these half-formed pictures. Do not try to analyse where the images are coming from or whether they are appropriate or not. This is simply time for you to relax and to allow notions of your character and their world to permeate your consciousness.

When you feel that you are ready, the facilitator will ask you to roll over on to one side and then to come slowly up to standing. Don't think about the experience you have just had, simply acknowledge the feelings that are alive in you.

The facilitator will now ask you to undertake a short, simple task. The entire company may be exploring different activities, but you will all work simultaneously so that there is no sense of this being in any way a performance. For instance, you might untie your shoelace and remove your shoe. You might sit down on a chair and then get up again. It doesn't matter as long as it is specific and achievable in the room and with the objects that you have available to you.

Before you begin exploring your task, take a moment to visualise your character doing it. What is she like rhythmically? Is she jerky as she completes the movement? Does she rush in or is there hesitancy in completing the action? How does he pick up his shoe? Does your character sink into the chair or perch bird-like on the edge of the seat?

As you visualise in detail your character's engagement with the task, undertake the activity yourself. Begin to embody the rhythms, with both yourself and the image of your character coming together to complete the physical action. Keep repeating the task so that, once you have removed your shoe, go back to neutral, put it back on your foot and then begin your visualisation again as you proceed once more with the action. Keep repeating so that you become very precise in what you are doing. Don't work to change the way you execute the task in any way; instead allow yourself to engage with it through an imaginative connection to how your character moves. You might find your rhythm changes, you might find an emotional connection with what you are doing, but any shifts or developments will arise from a careful visualisation rather than your own need to be playful.

+ Assorted objects

Skills

Awareness, Character, Physicality, Relaxation, Rhythm

Visualisation 2

This is a similar exercise to the previous one, but this time you will need to prepare for it. The exercise can work with everyone engaging in their tasks simultaneously, but you might find it useful to watch each other, in order to give you an insight into the behaviour of the other characters.

To prepare, you need to do a close reading of the text and note specific physical tasks that your character engages in. Obviously a character is in continuous action, so you must isolate those tasks specific to your character that are pivotal in the telling of the story. For example, you may have a scene during which your character does the washing up; they may mend a broken picture frame; they may tune a guitar. If it were necessary for your character to do these things in order for the narrative to move on, then they would be appropriate tasks for you to play with. All these activities could happen as part of the onstage action or they might be referred to in the text as having happened, although we do not actually see them taking place during the course of the play. Make sure that the tasks you isolate are physically active; that your character is actively *doing* something.

Choose the task that intrigues you the most. You will need to assemble all the objects necessary for you to complete it; for example a washing-up bowl, plates, water, cloth, tea towel, etc. There should be no miming.

Set up the space so that you can begin the task and then, as with the previous exercise, begin to visualise in detail your character engaging with it. So, for example, see their hands in the washing-up bowl, see them rub the dishes, see them lift a plate dripping from the water, see them lay it down to dry.

As you continue with the visualisation, begin to perform the task. As before, allow your visualisation of the character to inform the way that you move.

Now you will also have the given circumstances to consider. For instance, is your character resentful of having to wash up again? Is it freezing cold in the kitchen? Are they excited to be cleaning up because someone special is coming over? Have they just received some momentous news? Is the crockery they are washing valuable? All the information will come from the text itself. You need to incorporate this information into your visualisation and let it texture the way you engage with the task.

Keep your activity concise and achievable. If it doesn't take very long for you to complete, then reset yourself to neutral before repeating it. If your task takes longer, then explore it for the length of time you have available. Each actor should work on his or her task for fifteen minutes.

+ Preparation; props (optional)
Skills
Awareness, Character, Imagination, Physicality, Rhythm

Gesture

Gesture is a very powerful tool in unlocking a character's inner life. You can make deep connections through this exercise.

It is important firstly to experience the power of your own physicality in the space. From this you can develop the work so that it focuses on a specific character.

Spread yourselves out in the room so that you have enough space to move freely without bumping into anyone else.

Open your arms wide in a broad gesture. Stand with your feet wide apart. Use your whole body without becoming uncomfortable or straining your muscles. Occupy as much space as it is physically possible for you to do without experiencing tension.

Hold this stance for ten seconds then reset your body back to its neutral state.

Repeat the movement, imagining that you are growing larger and larger each time you spread your arms and legs wide. Return to a neutral state between each repetition.

Now do the opposite. Imagine that you are shrinking. Curl yourself inwards so that you occupy as little space as is comfortably possible. Again repeat this process, returning to neutral every ten seconds.

Notice the difference. Obviously these are opposing physical choices, but each will also have psychological resonances for you.

Return to the free, broad movements. As you do so, focus on your chest and imagine that it is your centre and that it generates all your impulses. Visualise this centre as being incredibly powerful. Now allow that power to spread up into your head, through your arms, into your hands. Drive it down through your pelvis, your legs, your feet, into your toes. Without experiencing any tension and without straining, let the feeling of strength radiate through your whole body.

Engage in some basic physical actions. Sit down and then stand up. Lie on the floor and then come upright again. Walk to one side of the room and then walk back. You can perform any physical task as long as it is simple. As you do so, imagine that all your movements stem from an impulse originated in the centre of your chest; you will experience an impulse to move before you commit to the movement itself.

After you have accomplished each movement, allow the energy situated in your chest to continue to flow from you. Even in stillness you radiate that energy in an outward flow.

Your body should now feel free and powerful, and you can begin to explore in terms of your character.

You can either explore a pivotal moment that your character experiences in a scene that you are working on, or you can step back and view your character in a broader sense, taking into account their journey through the play as a whole.

Without analysis or premeditation, you should try assuming a physical gesture that represents the inner life of your character, either in a specific moment or throughout the text. Make the gesture bold, really heighten it. The idea is not to be small or naturalistic but for you to extend physically. Hold the gesture for ten seconds before returning to neutral and repeating it again. Keep it simple and precise and repeat it exactly each time. If you find that your impulse is to change the gesture because your previous exploration has not expressed what you wish it to, then do so. However, make sure that you have explored the initial gesture fully before altering it.

Here are some examples in order to clarify the exercise.

- My character is wracked with guilt because of something she has done: *I bow my head, turn my feet inwards and wring my hands.*
- My character is appealing for justice: *I extend my arms up to the heavens, spreading my fingers and lifting my gaze to follow my hands.*

- My character wants to protect a loved one: *I bend over cradling an imaginary baby in my arms.*
- My character feels oppressed: *I step forward and extend my palms out in front of me as if I am pressing against some invisible wall.*

Other than keeping the gestures simple and full and informed by evidence from the text, there are no rules here. You will find your own impulse for movement.

Having gone through the physical gesture several times, notice any psychological impact that it is having on you. This is a fantastic way of connecting to a character without having to dredge up feelings from deep inside, or to force anything emotionally. It is a useful exercise to do as a way of embodying your character's inner life during rehearsal, but it can also be used prior to an entrance into a scene, or between takes if you are on set. It will give you an immediate emotional connection to bring into the space. The energy will be flowing out of you, and you won't have had to spend time searching internally for an emotion, causing you to retreat inwards rather than radiating energy out of you where it can reach the other actors in the scene – and those watching it.

Skills

Awareness, Energy, Inner life, Physicality

Forces

Do a close reading of the scene, or a moment in the script that you want to explore.

Decide on the factors that have an effect on your character, not only those present in the scene itself, but also those that are invisible. In other words, what forces are working on your character as they engage with the action of the text?

In order to do this, you will need to consider the circumstances of the scene within the context of the play as a whole and what you know has been going on for your character.

For example, the circumstances of the scene I am exploring are as follows:

- The character I am playing is a lecturer. It is nine o'clock at night during winter. He has stayed late at work to concentrate on a book he is writing and needs to finish, but he has just been joined in his office by a student who is struggling with an essay that she is finding difficult. He knows that she finds him attractive and that her difficulty with the work is just a pretext so that she can be alone with him. He also really fancies her.
- His wife has taken their baby son to stay with her mother so that he can focus on his work for the week. He loves his wife, but since the birth of their baby six months ago their sex life has dwindled radically. He is resentful and feels that they were too young to start having children.
- This is his first job since graduating, and he wants to do well in it. He is ambitious and already has his eye on promotion.
- There may be other tutors still in the college working late.
- During the scene he kisses the student.

Having considered the given circumstances I will now identify the most pressing forces that are at work on my character during the scene.

- *Force 1: His student.* My character is drawn to her physically. He urgently wants to kiss her.

- *Force 2: His wife.* My character loves his wife and she trusts him.
- *Force 3: His baby.* My character is a father now and as such feels a responsibility towards his child.
- *Force 4: His ambition.* If my character has sex with the student and anyone in authority finds out, he will, at the very least, be overlooked for promotion, but most likely dismissed.
- *Force 5: His faith.* If my character gives in to temptation, he will be committing adultery, which he considers a sin.

In this way select the forces that you believe are working on your character during the scene that you are exploring.

If there are enough people present, then use them to represent each force. So for my scenario I would choose people to represent my character's wife, child, ambition and faith. Obviously the student is in the scene with me and will work on me directly so needs no representation. If there are not enough people present during the exercise then write the name of each force down on separate sheets of paper.

Position the people or pieces of paper in the room. Using my example, I might place *my wife* just behind me. *My baby* might be in my sightline to one side. *My ambition* might be seated at my desk. *My faith* might be posted further away just by the door.

Once you have positioned your forces there is no need to do anything further with them other than to allow them to work on you. If you are using people to represent your forces they do not need to do anything except to occupy the space in which they have been placed and to watch what is going on. The point is that they are present for your character during the scene. They are silent witnesses to the choices he makes as dictated by the script.

As you play the scene, allow yourself to be affected by the forces that surround you. Your point of concentration can move between them as they come in and out of the foreground of your attention. For example, in my scenario I might find myself pulled towards the student I fancy, but then feel the presence of my wife at my shoulder witnessing my betrayal. I might catch a glimpse of my faith even in the act of kissing my student. You may find that one force is more dominant than another; this is a useful way of determining what is most important to your character at any given point. The exercise works to show you the forces pushing and pulling, creating conflicts for you to explore and sparking the inner life of your character.

+ Preparation; paper and a pen (optional)

Skills

Conflict, Focus, Imagination, Inner life

Inner Monologue

This exercise is not about writing beautifully. It is about using your imagination in order to discover an essence of a character that might not be immediately apparent from the text.

After a close reading of the play, note down five qualities or characteristics that you associate with your character. These do not necessarily come from what other characters say about you. For example, another character might describe you as 'money-grabbing', but you know that your character grew up in poverty and is terrified of ever experiencing that again. In the light of this, rather than describing your character as 'money-grabbing', you might choose to describe him as 'frightened' instead. All your choices should come from information gleaned from the play, but your imagination needs to sift through them so that you can begin to uncover the essence of the character you are playing. You don't need to note every possible facet of their personality; focus on the five that seem most vibrant and intriguing to you as an actor.

Write a monologue that is two to three minutes in length. The time frame of this monologue is that it occurs within a year of the start of the play.

This monologue is *not* a character biography. You do not need to set up a backdrop or personal history for your character. It should speak of an experience. This can be as small as sitting on a red-velvet chair to wait for a friend and hearing a clock strike, or of eating a piece of chocolate cake that was delicious. It could incorporate smells and touch and the quality of the light. How is your character feeling at that moment? What does your character really want? How does your character view the world? Is your character afraid of something? Again, your choices will originate from information gleaned from the text, but your imagination will play with them to explore elements that the script does not describe explicitly.

That world needs to be specific. Where is your character at this moment? What time is it? What have they just been doing? What is the weather like? What are they doing now? Set up your space accordingly. For example, perhaps your character is taking off her make-up after a night out. She is in her bedroom. It is very late, outside it is raining hard and she is cold in her room. She has just been to a restaurant with her fiancé. Over the course of the meal he has told her that their four-year relationship is over because he no longer finds her exciting. She suspects that another woman is involved, and she wants to find out who she is so that she can confront her. She is convinced that if she can only talk to the woman she can persuade her to leave her fiancé alone.

These choices will not be random but will have resulted from clues or references found in the play itself. For example, the play might make reference to the fact that your character is still in love with a man who no longer wants her. However, the monologue speaks of what your character is thinking at this moment, a moment that takes place before the play begins as she takes her make-up off alone in this cold room with only the noise of the rain to keep her company.

Learn the monologue. In its delivery you should draw on the five characteristics or personal qualities that you chose earlier. You can explore these physically, through rhythm and tempo, through the way you hold yourself, through the energy your character radiates. These qualities should be apparent in your character's relationship to the world around them through the course of the monologue.

Do not simply stand in the middle of the room and deliver your speech. Create the atmosphere, make it active. Bring in any props that you need to be able to do that.

+ Preparation; props (optional)

Skills

Analysis, Character, Imagination, Rhythm

Atmosphere

I have included work on atmosphere in Part Two because how our character behaves will be affected by the mood of a place or a situation, a relationship or a piece of news. Different characters will have different responses to that mood. As an actor you should never play these moods or atmospheres as such, but that is not to say that your character is not sensitive to them. Here are some examples:

- The mood/atmosphere of a family gathering might be charged with warmth, with an air of hope and celebration for your character.
- The mood/atmosphere of a specific room might be claustrophobic and oppressive to your character.
- The mood/atmosphere between characters might be laced with tension and recrimination.

Remember the atmosphere might not be the same for each character. Your character might have a different response to those around them; one person's feeling of imprisonment might signify liberation to another.

Having located the section of the text that you want to use for this exercise, consider the mood or atmosphere that you think is most dominant for your character during that exchange of dialogue.

Imagine that, as you breathe, you are inhaling the atmosphere you have chosen to explore. Imagine that the air around you is brimming with mood. It is as if each molecule of oxygen is formed by it, and as you inhale you are filling your lungs with more and more of the atmosphere surrounding you. Imagine that, as that air touches your skin, you are supremely sensitive to it. As you imagine the atmosphere becoming increasingly charged, you in turn are being charged by it. A good example of how atmosphere affects people is to think about what happens during a seance. Participants become filled with excitement, fear, dread or anticipation. The air around them becomes impregnated with these sensations as though it is a living thing, feeding off the emotions in the room, and also fuelling them.

When you are sure that you can not only imagine the atmosphere around you, but can also maintain it, begin to relate the reaction inside of you to the imaginary atmosphere outside of you. Do not force anything to happen, but rather allow it to develop and build naturally.

Now you can begin to move and speak in response to the atmosphere you have created. Play the scene accordingly.

Let's imagine that the scene you are working on involves a family celebration. The atmosphere in the room is one of warmth and joy. Your character's father has just got a job after months of unemployment. This is an opportunity for the family to look to the future with optimism.

Your character has just been diagnosed with a rare form of bone cancer and has six months to live. No one else in the family knows this devastating information yet. The knowledge of his illness will clearly inform your character's behavior. Although the script dictates that he joins in with the celebrations, what might the mood of the event actually be for him? Is the atmosphere for him charged with sadness? Fear? Anger? Regret? How does he move and speak in relation to it?

You should explore the atmosphere fully, although in the final playing of the scene your choices may be far subtler. Through this exercise you will not only be able to explore how an atmosphere affects you physically and emotionally, but also how characters exploring different atmospheres meet points of conflict. Remember this is not about *playing* a mood but rather being *responsive* to the mood of a place, event or relationship.

+ Preparation

Skills

Awareness, Imagination, Responsiveness

What If?

This exercise allows you to understand the gap between the character's needs and the reality of their situation. By changing elements of the scene it also gives you an insight into how your character might behave differently if their circumstances and relationships with other characters were different.

Having read the scene as it is written out loud together, and allowed yourself time for a brief discussion, you will then improvise as much of the dialogue as is necessary to bring about the required changes. Establish the given circumstances of the scene, the time, place, what has just happened, etc. Everything about the scene can be kept as written, except that you are now at liberty to exercise the magic 'What if?' – what if things happened differently?

You can repeat the scene as many times as necessary, but each time you can only make *one* alteration to the circumstances, and you can only make that alteration in relation to *one* of the character's desires. In order to do this, you might be able to stick to the actual dialogue of the script, using your own words only when you reach the point where you aim for a different outcome to that which is written, or you might find it necessary to improvise the whole scene, creating the dialogue throughout. Don't add unnecessary elements; as much as possible you should adhere to the narrative drive of the scene.

Here's an example. Through my reading of the text I understand that my character wants other people to respect her. She feels that she is just as remarkable as her other family members, but that they do not value her qualities or notice how funny or interesting she is.

The given circumstances of the scene are that it is my character's eldest sister's birthday and the family is gathered for a celebratory meal. It is an evening in summer, and everyone is dressed up for the occasion. During the scene, my character's father gives a speech reminiscing about my sister's life, telling anecdotes about what a funny and charming little girl she was and reflecting on what a wonderful adult she has become. Everyone has been drinking and chipping in with their own memories. There is much laughter and warmth around the table. Towards the end of the scene, having imbibed a little too much wine, my character gets the courage to tell a story about a time she and her sister had decided to run away from home. They had got as far as the end of the road when her sister had got a stomach ache and the adventure had had to be aborted. My character's intention is to make everyone laugh and in doing so to gain some attention.

In the scene as written after my character has told the story there is a pause in which everyone falls silent before her mother asks her why she always has to bring something negative to the proceedings?

The *change* I want to make is that instead of finding the story offensive, the rest of the family find it hilarious and the conversation turns to stories involving my character's own pursuits as a little girl.

We play the scene as written until the pivotal moment when my character tells her story. Then, instead of following the script, the other actors improvise; they laugh appreciatively and begin to recount funny little incidents involving my character as a child. My character can now bask in the glow of the warmth and attention that she lacks in the actual text. As an actor this gives me a chance to really understand what my character is missing, and strengthens my insight into how much she needs that recognition. When I return to the scene as written, this understanding will inform my behaviour as the character.

Skills

Character, Imagination, Inner life

Music

Music can be used in all sorts of ways when approaching character. This exercise explores the effect the rhythm and tempo of a piece of music has on you physically. You will find that the by-product of exploring in this way is that emotions will be triggered in you and that your connection to your character will be deepened.

All the actors in the group engage with this exercise simultaneously.

Select a piece of music that you feel speaks to your character either in general through the play or during a specific point in the text. Do not choose music with lyrics as these can begin to do the work for you. Select a piece that you feel reflects the journey of your character through the play or corresponds with your character's inner workings during a particular moment or scene within it. Pay particular attention to the rhythms of the music and its tempo. Consider too the atmosphere it evokes for you.

Some examples:

- My character feels trapped and claustrophobic. Throughout the course of the play she tries to escape her circumstances, but is ultimately unable to do so, as they pull her back, preventing her from moving on with her life. In reflection of this, the music I choose loops back on itself, returning to an insistent rhythm that it does not ever seem fully to break from. To help you get an idea of what I mean, listen to some Spanish guitar flamenco music.
- My character is constantly contemplating the past and wishing he had made different choices in his life. The music I choose is laced for me with an atmosphere of nostalgia and regret. For example, the Adagietto from Mahler's *Fifth Symphony*.
- My character is unsettled and angry. She cannot forgive a wrong that has been done her. The music that I choose is powerful, the beat abrupt and insistent. Perhaps Stravinsky's *The Firebird*.

- My character has just confessed his love for someone, only to discover that his feelings are requited. The music that I choose is fast-paced and rhythmic and makes me want to dance when I listen to it. Think about Beethoven's *Ode to Joy*.
- My character has found out that her best friend has betrayed her by sleeping with the man she loves. As a result she is consumed by bewilderment and rage. The music I choose reflects this chaos of anger and hurt. It soars to a peak or crescendo before crashing away then rising to swell again. Listen to Rachmaninoff's *Symphony No. 1 in D minor* for a sense of this.

Throughout each stage of this exercise you will listen to the music you have chosen through headphones. You are going to move so these will need to be connected to something portable. If the piece of music ends before the exercise does then you will simply play it again as many times as is required.

Find a space in the room and lie down or sit on the floor listening to your music. Allow yourself enough time to let it affect you. Do not force any response to the music, simply let yourself be receptive to its rhythms, tempos and atmosphere. When you feel ready, start to explore your relationship to the music physically. What effect is the music having on your body? How does your body respond to this effect in terms of the way it makes you want to move?

Now begin to move around the room continuing to listen to your music. Find a chair and sit on it. Stand up and cross the room. Open a window or a door. Lean against a wall. You can move wherever you want to and in whatever manner that the music suggests to you. You might run, stop abruptly, then run again. You might drift over the floor or roll across it, or dance in a corner. Your movements could be sensual or jerky. Your music might make you spin or twitch, glide or creep. You must not anticipate how you will respond or try to create a logical narrative for your movements. Simply submit to any impulse that you have to move – and allow for any psychological effects that might materialise as a result of your physical responses to the music.

Having begun to fully embody the impulses triggered by your music, you can now begin to work in relation to anyone else in the room. You might find yourself drawn to another character and their presence will be a further stimulus to the way you move. You may find that you want to remain solitary, you may find you want to avoid somebody. The way you move might harmonise with another's movements, or it may work in opposing rhythms to that person. It is about allowing the music and the presence of another character to work on you without you feeling the need to impose a narrative on what you are doing, or to justify it logically. The exercise should continue long enough to facilitate your absorption of the rhythms, tempos, tones and textures of your music so that you are able to respond to it physically – and, as a by-product, psychologically – without your conscious mind working to censor or analyse in any way.

Note

You could apply this exercise to a specific scene, using the text as well as the music. If it is a duologue that you are working on, then stand facing the other actor involved. Both of you listen to your own music through your headphones. Allow the music to inform you, and start to speak the dialogue of the scene, each actor speaking in turn as the script dictates. After a few lines, take off one of the headphones so that the music is not such a strong presence in your ears. Continue until you feel ready to remove the remaining headphone, and carry on with the rest of the text. You should have a sense of what the rhythm, tempo, atmosphere and emotion of the music awakened in you as you interact with the other actor in the scene.

+ Preparation; pieces of recorded music

Skills

Awareness, Inner life, Physicality, Rhythm

PART THREE

TEXT

Peter Brook said that 'A word does not start as a word. It is an end product which begins as an impulse, stimulated by attitude and behaviours which dictate the need for expression' (*The Empty Space*).

The games and exercises in Part Three aim to help you to unlock text in order to explore that expression. I have not specified that any exercise is more suited to a particular genre or style than another. They can be applied to and adapted for a variety of scripts. Your freedom to play with text, to realise it and connect to it is the focus of the chapter.

I have grouped the games into sections. However, as is the case with all the exercises contained in this book, there will be overlaps. For some of the exercises, actors will need to be off-book, with their lines memorised, and others simply require a familiarity with the text.

As mentioned previously, I switch between addressing the facilitator and the actor, in order to clarify certain exercises. The role of the teacher/director/workshop leader, should, however, be clear throughout.

Connection

The following exercises are aimed at helping the actor to bring the text to life in a way that is personal to them. They also work to free the actor when they are struggling to communicate or feeling inhibited.

Whispering the Text

Sit back to back with the person you have a scene with, making sure that you are making contact with them physically. Go through the text together, whispering the lines to each other. The fact that you are sitting back to back allows you to experience the words passed between you physically.

Repeat the exercise, but this time stand close to the people you are in the scene with, facing them. Whisper the text to each other, but this time, instead of communicating to each other physically through your backs, the words are whispered through space to reach their target.

Skills
Communication, Focus, Physicality

Singing the Text

Quite simply, instead of speaking the text, sing it.

If you want to work for release in particular, then sing the text in different styles: opera, folk, rock, etc.

Do not try and sing sweetly, or be tuneful. Just sing out and release the words, letting the tune and the rhythm take care of themselves.

Skills

Communication, Focus, Relaxation, Rhythm

Drawing the Text

Make sure that you understand the meaning of the speech before you begin the exercise.

On a large sheet of paper, draw an image for every word of the text, even the little words like 'of', 'and', 'but'. You do not have to draw literal images, as that would be difficult with these joining words, you can use a symbol, shape or dash to express them.

Do this exercise slowly, allowing yourself to mull over each word before you commit it to paper. This is not a free-association exercise; it requires careful thought.

When you have finished, you should be able to see how all the images you have drawn work to form the speech as a whole. You do not need to be good at drawing to do the exercise; whether your pictures are well crafted or not is irrelevant. When you come to speak the words you will have made them personal and specific to you, with a visual image of them in your mind.

+ Paper and a pen

Skills

Communication, Imagination

Breathing the Line

This exercise is adapted from the work of acting coach Harold Guskin.

Read from your script slowly, taking one section at a time. This section could be as short as a single word, a line, or it might stretch to a phrase. When you have isolated the beat of the text you are looking at, read it over to yourself, inhaling deeply as you do so. Let yourself be absorbed by the word or words. As soon as you get an image or thought or sensation in relation to what you have read, look up, exhale and then speak the text out loud. When you have done this, look back at your script and inhale the next word, line or phrase. When you feel a response to it, again look up, exhale and speak the text aloud. Continue through the text in this way.

Do not censor or analyse your response to the words. If you repeat the exercise, you may find that you respond differently each time. Make sure you always exhale before you speak. If you feel nothing when you read your phrase, then that is a response in itself, and how you speak the words will be textured by it.

Note

This exercise moves the text with the breath and allows you to access fresh responses to the words you speak each time you say them. You may discover responses that surprise you, but that may be useful in relation to a deepening sense of your character and an understanding of the words that they choose to say. It will break you out of set patterns and rhythms of speech that perhaps you have fallen into.

+ Your script

Skills

Analysis, Breathing, Communication, Responsiveness, Rhythm

Free Association

First Version: Key Phrases

Key phrases in this context mean the things that your character says that you believe are of real importance to them.

On a sheet of paper, taking one scene at a time, write a list of the key phrases that your character says. Use the exact words that the playwright has given you, do not paraphrase. If the context is unclear, then write in brackets beside the line what the character is referring to. Do not write down everything, but concentrate instead on the most pressing issues for your character.

For example, consider the exercise in the light of the following exchange that I have written for clarification purposes. Imagine that you are playing Character A.

> A. I'm not going. Don't try to persuade me.
>
> B. It will be fun. All those people you haven't seen for years.
>
> A. You don't understand. Those people will have got older and that will remind me that I have got older. All school reunions do is make you feel inadequate. At school I was so shiny. Captain of the netball team, star of the school plays, grade-A student. I was the girl who was going to do something with her life. Hayley James, Emma Lock, Kirsty Strong. They will all have achieved more than I have.
>
> B. John will be there.
>
> A. He doesn't love me any more.

The list of key phrases from Character A's point of view might be as follows:

- *I am not going.*
- *You don't understand.*
- *I have got older.*
- *Make you feel inadequate. (School reunions.)*
- *I was so shiny.*

- *I was the girl who was going to do something with her life.*
- *They will have achieved more than I have.*
- *He doesn't love me any more.*

Now, from the list that you have made, select which phrases are the most provocative for you; which phrases do you as an actor have a gut reaction to? Having done this, write one of them down at the top of a sheet of paper.

For example, from my list I am going to choose: '*I was so shiny.*'

Close your eyes and repeat the provocative statement to yourself until it starts to have an effect on you. When this happens, open your eyes, and below where you have written it, write a free association that follows on from that statement. Use '*I*' not the character's name. What you write should be informed by your close reading of the whole script, but there are no rules: any image, thought or feeling that arises should be written without censorship. Do not use any punctuation and do not pause to think about what you are writing. Fill the page with a stream of consciousness stimulated by your key phrase, like this example:

> *I was so shiny:*
> Christmas reds blues golds lights bright pebbles in water with sunlight on them the sun and stars and I glowed and people looked at me they looked up to me because I shimmered mermaid's tails swishing hair swishing when I walked people grouped around me wanting to be like me wanting to shine like me meteorites the brightest star in a dark sky wrapping paper with silky bows new dress new shoes boldness crystal diamonds glitter I glitter in other people's eyes…

Your piece will be longer, but as you can see from this, there is no need to worry about whether what you write makes sense to anyone else. Your own private connection to the words is what matters. The words of the text must be personal and specific to you, and this exercise offers you a way of allowing that to happen. You should go through all your key phrases in this way. Keep returning to the exercise throughout your rehearsals as your understanding of the character deepens.

Second Version: Key Facts

Repeat the exercise, but this time focus on all the things, people and places that your character refers to in the script. Under your heading for each one write a free association as you did with the key phrases.

Using the previous example dialogue, the list of facts that I would make would be as follows:

- *School*
- *Netball team*
- *School plays*
- *Grade-A student*
- *Hayley James*
- *Emma Lock*
- *Kirsty Strong*
- *John*

Begin with the fact that you find the most provocative, repeating it until you are affected by it and then, without pause or punctuation, write down any thoughts, images or emotions that it has evoked for you. For example:

> *School:*
> Corridors peeling walls pinboards loose paper doors gymnasium white with climbing bars and blue mats chalk on blackboard yellow wood desks ladles tin trays white plates clatter noise concrete window hooks grey maroon showers green field tennis courts mean girls pushing teacher standing headmaster's office blue chairs prefect's badge puckering V-neck jumper disco boys friends rain coach fights bags swinging mustard paint stairs lace-up shoes belonging wanting familiar hot damp gates…

You may find that you write less for the key facts, but you can add more every time you revisit the exercise.

Third Version: Key Doings

Repeat the exercise, but rather than write anything down, you are going to speak your thoughts out loud.

Consider what your character needs in the scene you are working on. Think of this need in terms of their deepest wish, the thing that propels them through the action and informs their choices.

Using the short scene from the earlier parts of the exercise, I believe that Character A needs to feel that she has made something of her life. This need is born from the fear that she considers herself a failure since she left school. Now consider what your character is *doing* to the person he or she is talking to. Select the main action, the key doing, that your character is playing in relation to what you have decided is their deeper wish.

Returning to my scene, I believe that Character A wants her friend to contradict her. She is appealing to her friend to tell her that she has done alright in her life, that she still shines. Think of a situation in your own life when you did something that mirrors the key doing of your character. Obviously the situation may have been quite different; as would be the person you were talking to at that time. You can choose something that took place a very long time ago or something more recent.

In this example, Character A's key doing: *To appeal for reassurance.*

A parallel situation from my own life: The time I appealed to the man I loved to tell me that he still wanted me. My suspicions were that he had fallen in love with someone else.

Begin the scene, playing the text as written. When the facilitator claps their hands, switch to your own words as you explore the key doing in relation to the parallel incident from your own life. Speak to the other person as if they were the person from your own life. You can use their name. When the facilitator claps their hands again, return to the text. Keep switching back and forth between the script and your own words each time you hear the facilitator clap. Commit fully to the key doing throughout; make sure you have chosen something where the stakes are high enough. Don't censor what you say. Let yourself speak without thought. If you run out of words then simply repeat the key doing until more come to you.

Here is an example using my own script:

> You don't understand. These people will have got older and that reminds me that I have got older. [*The facilitator claps.*] *I want you to look at me and tell me that you love me. Don't just say it, mean it. What do you see when you look at me, do you think I am attractive? Do you still want to go to bed with me? Look at me and tell me you love me. You don't like me any more, do you? You think I look ugly, don't you? You think I'm boring, don't you? I appeal to you... I appeal to you. I appeal to you...* [*The facilitator claps.*] All school reunions do is make you feel inadequate. At school I was so shiny. [*The facilitator claps.*] *I appeal to you... You used to laugh at my jokes, don't you think I am funny any more? Tell me that I am funny. Please, tell me you love me. I don't want you to leave me. Say that you are staying...*

Go through your own script in this way until you have explored the key doing, both in terms of the text and your own connection with it through an event in your own life.

+ Paper and a pen

Skills

Analysis, Communication, Imagination, Inner life

Clarification

These exercises aim to clarify the text, either when the actor is getting too caught up in their emotional connection to it, or when it is particularly dense and so needs unpicking. They will enable the actor to see what they are talking about and to whom at any given point.

Said the...

Play the scene, but after every full line of text say '*Said the man*' or '*Said the woman*'.

For example:

A. 'I want you to leave now.'

ACTOR PLAYING A. *Said the woman.*

B. 'Where am I supposed to go?'

ACTOR PLAYING B. *Said the man.*

This exercise helps to distance you when the emotions are becoming overwhelming and obscuring the text.

Skills

Conflict, Focus, Inner life

Targeting the Text

As you speak each line of your text, consider it in the light of the following questions:

- Am I saying this line in order to achieve something for myself? If so, what is it that I want to achieve and why?
- Am I saying this line for the benefit of another character? If so, what do I want to do for or to them? Do I want to please them? Do I want to give them some information? Do I want to propel them into action?
- Am I saying this line for the benefit of the audience? Do I need to deliver some particular information? Do I want to provoke them?
- Is the apparent beneficiary of this line actually the person it claims to be directed to? For instance, I may be ostensibly talking to one character, but in fact my character is trying to make an impression on or give information to another character. I may be speaking a line to myself, but in fact I need the information contained within it to have a particular resonance with the audience.

You can play around with each line, targeting a different recipient each time.

Skills

Character, Focus, Inner life

Chair-Hopping

Arrange the chairs so that they are placed at intervals around the room.

The actors involved in the scene will sit in chairs and begin to speak the text. Every time there is a change of thought, the speaker moves to another chair and sits on it. Only move between the lines and be careful not to move unnecessarily.

Often, although the subject seems to have changed, the text is actually still dealing with the original thought, but simply approaching it from a different angle. If you find that you are hopping from chair to chair between each line this could be a textual indicator of the state of your character's mind. This exercise is an excellent way of revealing the underlying through line of a speech or scene.

+ Lots of chairs

Skills

Analysis, Focus, Inner life, Physicality

Repeating the Text

Play the scene.

Each actor can repeat any line or word or phrase that they hear spoken because they feel they need to unpick it further. Maybe it is central to the exchange, is pertinent to their character, or maybe its meaning remains ambiguous.

Once that line, word or phrase has been repeated, the actor who originally spoke it must say it again. The repetition of the text will continue back and forth until both actors are satisfied that it has been dealt with, at which point the dialogue resumes as normal.

You should repeat lines or words or phrases that you find particularly resonant, or which you do not fully understand. Only move on with the next section of text when you feel that you have explored the word or phrase fully through the repetition. You do not need to repeat everything you hear.

Skills

Analysis, Awareness, Focus

Cups

For this exercise you will need a stack of paper cups. The number of cups will depend on the number of references the character makes to people, ideas and events within the speech.

On the base of each paper cup write a title for the subject that it will represent; you could use a different colour pen for each title. The 'title' could simply be the name of a person or place, or it could be more complex, referring to a situation, action or need.

Consider the following short speech that I have written as an example:

> I can smell the sea still, even here. I can feel the fresh tang of salt in the air, even through the petrol fumes of the city. I can see my mother waiting for me, standing by the lace curtains at the window, looking out at the empty lane. Our seaside home, with its crumbling fence and the paint peeling around the door frame. The sound of the sea audible through its solid stone walls. He touches me and I can hear the gulls screeching after the fishing boats. He leads me through the city and my feet nudge the shingle of the shore. The guilt I feel, and the lust and the longing for home and the desire to be away, combine in our kiss.

For each element of this speech I am going to write on a cup. Here is what I might write:

Cup 1: *The Sea*

Cup 2: *The City*

Cup 3: *My Mother*

Cup 4: *My Childhood Home*

Cup 5: *The Man*

Cup 6: *My Guilt*

Cup 7: *My Lust*

Cup 8: *Homesickness*

Cup 9: *The Need to Escape*

Cup 10: *The Kiss*

Place the cups around the space that you are working in, with the base visible so that you can see the title which is written there. As you go through the speech aloud, pick up the cup that corresponds to whatever it is that you are talking about.

When you are no longer talking about that particular thing, then put the cup back down. If you are talking about more than one thing at once, you may keep hold of as many cups as you need.

Using the above speech, when I mention *My Mother* I will obviously pick up the cup with that written on it, but I may also choose to hold the cup marked *Guilt* as well. When I pick up the cup with *The Man* written on it on the line '*He touches me*', I might also feel the need to pick up the cup marked *Lust*.

There might be an occasion when although you are apparently talking about one subject, you have an impulse to pick up a cup with something different on it. For example, perhaps when I talk about *The City*, I pick up the cup with *Homesickness* written on it instead. This exercise helps you to understand and make specific the elements of the text and the things your character is thinking about and responding to.

+ Paper cups and a pen

Skills

Awareness, Focus, Multitasking

Rhythm

By exploring the rhythms of language, actors can gain access to the emotional undercurrents that pulse through it. Rather like a musical score, the rhythms of the text combine to create the whole. Through them, the meaning of the words hold a deeper significance and the relationships between those speaking them become clearer.

Beating Out the Rhythm

It is useful to wear blindfolds for this exercise as this helps to shut out distractions, enabling everyone to focus solely on the rhythms – and the responses that these rhythms elicit in them. If you are working on a monologue then find a space in the room to sit alone. If you are exploring a scene or a particular exchange then sit with the other actors involved in it. You will need to be off-book for this exercise.

Put on your blindfolds.

You are going to play the scene or monologue, but instead of using words, you are going to beat out the rhythms of the text. You can use your hands and feet. You can tap gently or knock loudly. You can sit in the silences between the words and phrases. The rhythms you use can communicate with and respond to those created by the other actors in the scene. It is important that you do not anticipate what you are going to do. Work in the moment off your impulses. Do not feel you have to make a sound for every word or try to devise a clear narrative. You are exploring essences here to glean a deeper meaning. Allow yourself to become absorbed in the abstract nature of the exercise.

Note

It is possible that actors can become 'lost', not knowing where the other actor or actors are in the text. You will have to be very sensitive to each other, and listen intently. If it becomes muddled, then stop what you are doing, locate a place in the script from which to pick up, and then continue with the exercise.

+ Blindfolds

Skills

Awareness, Communication, Rhythm

Sharing the Text

Everyone sits in a circle on the floor, close to one another. Choose a speech or monologue to be explored – it helps if everyone has learnt it in advance, but if not, have it written out clearly in front of each player. If you do know it then you can do this exercise blindfolded.

The speech begins when the first player in the circle says the first word of it, the actor sitting to their right speaks the next, and so it continues around the circle, with each player taking a single word of the text when it is their turn to do so. If the monologue hasn't finished by the time it is the turn of the first player again, then continue round, working right through to the end of the speech. If the monologue finishes before everyone in the circle has had a chance to say a word, then begin again and keep going round until everyone has contributed. It is a good idea to work through the speech a number of times anyway so that everyone can become familiar with it and can listen out for the rhythms highlighted by this sharing of the text. The idea is that the whole group works as if with one voice.

Catch the word from the previous person and pass it on to the next in a continuous flow. Allow for the rhythms to build and to jolt, to increase in speed and to slow down. Be aware also where the pauses in the text fall. They are as much part of the rhythm of the whole as the words are.

+ Blindfolds (optional)

Skills

Collaboration, Focus, Rhythm

Passing a Ball

The actors play the scene, but as they do so, they pass a ball to whoever it is that they are talking to.

The ball can be thrown, rolled, dribbled or bounced between actors. It can even be placed gently into another character's hands.

If it is your turn to speak and you are not in possession of the ball, then simply take it from the person who has it, and pass it on to the person you are about to address. The speed with which the ball passes between the actors, and the manner in which it does so, indicates what is happening rhythmically within the scene.

+ A ball

Skills

Awareness, Responsiveness, Rhythm

Punctuation

Choose a speech in which to explore the rhythm of the punctuation. Begin to read through the speech aloud. When you are actually speaking stand still, but when you come across a punctuation mark walk a little way. Every time you hit a punctuation mark, travel in a different direction to the way you were previously walking.

Punctuation marks can be used as a steer through the rhythms and the ideas of a speech. As such, they also serve as a useful indicator for the psychological state of the character. If you are becoming dizzy switching directions every few words, then it is likely that this mirrors the unsettled emotional state of the character you are playing.

Skills

Communication, Inner life, Rhythm

70

TEXT

No Punctuation

Begin your speech, but this time proceed as though there was no punctuation at all. It might be useful to copy the speech down first on a piece of paper removing all of the punctuation. You can then use this to read from which may be easier.

Notice where you need to breathe as you read the speech. Discover your own sense of the rhythm through the words, without being dictated to by the restrictions of the punctuation. You should find that you take a breath every time the thought changes, and this will guide you through the music of the text.

+ Paper and a pen

Skills

Analysis, Breathing, Rhythm

Actions

The following exercises and games all revolve around the playing of actions. On stage, as in life, we are always *doing* something in order to achieve our purpose, however mundane that may be. Sometimes in life we are unaware of our actions even in the act of executing them. When working on a script, however, it is useful to map out the actions that our character uses, in order to be specific and to illuminate our passage through the text.

An action can be both physical and psychological. The two are linked. My character picks up a teapot. My character pours tea into a cup. My character sits down. This is an outline of what my character is doing *physically*. The sequence of physical actions triggers an accompanying *psychological* response. In turn, the way my character feels will inform the way my character performs the physical actions; it will texture and direct their behaviour. An action is always in a response to a need.

Physicalising the Action

Begin by outlining the given circumstances of the scene that you are working on.

Play the scene, but allocate the lines to readers who are not playing the roles.

As each character's line is spoken by the reader, the actor must touch someone else in the scene. The way they touch that person must correspond to the action of the line that is being read out (by 'action', I mean what you are doing to another person). The person receiving the contact is not necessarily the person being spoken to directly; sometimes, although we appear to be talking to one person, the action we are playing through the line is actually intended for someone else's benefit. Here are three examples:

1) The scene takes place on a hospital ward. My character's girlfriend has been involved in a nasty car accident, which has left her disfigured. He is visiting her for the first time since the accident.

READER 1 (*speaking my girlfriend's line*). Don't look at me.

The actor playing my girlfriend puts her hand over my eyes.

ACTION: To *shield* her boyfriend from seeing the extent of the disfigurement.

READER 2 (*speaking my line*). You look beautiful.

I gently remove her hand from my face and stroke it.

ACTION: To *reassure* my girlfriend that I still love her.

READER 3 (*speaking the nurse's line*). She's very tired.

The actor playing the nurse puts her hand firmly on my shoulder.

ACTION: To *warn* me that this isn't going to be easy.

This is one version of events, but there will be others that you can play with as you repeat the scene. For example:

READER 1. Don't look at me.

The actor playing my girlfriend reaches up and draws my face close to hers.

ACTION: To *test* her boyfriend's continued attraction for her.

READER 2. You look beautiful.

I cross to the nurse and stroke her face.

ACTION: To *seduce* the nurse.

READER 3. She's very tired.

The actor playing the nurse drifts her hand down my chest.

ACTION: To *invite* me to leave the room with her.

2) I am at an office party with a work colleague who has just been promoted above me, and our boss who gave her that promotion.

READER 1 (*speaking my line*). Congratulations.

I give the actor playing my colleague a hug.

ACTION: To *befriend* my colleague during a time of possible tension between us.

READER 2 (*speaking my colleague's line*). You should have got it.

The actor playing my colleague puts her hands on my shoulders and looks me straight in the eye.

ACTION: To *bolster* me in case I am feeling deflated.

READER 3 (*speaking my boss's line*). It was a close-run thing.

The actor playing my boss shakes my hand firmly.

ACTION: To *encourage* me not to give up.

Alternatively:

READER 1. Congratulations.

I grab my boss's lapels aggressively.

ACTION: To *threaten* my boss, having been overlooked for promotion.

READER 2. You should have got it.

The actor playing my colleague goes and stands behind the actor playing my boss.

ACTION: To *appeal* for some protection in the event of an attack.

READER 3. It was a close-run thing.

The actor playing my boss puts her arm around the actor playing my colleague.

ACTION: To *support* her employee.

3) I am at the start line of a running race. The man and woman beside me look really fit, and I know I haven't put in enough hours of training.

READER 1 (*speaking the female runner's line*). Let's run together.

The actor playing this role links one of her arms through mine.

ACTION: To *enlist* my support ahead of a really long race.

READER 2 (*speaking my line*). I don't think I can do it.

I clasp the female runner's hand really tightly.

ACTION: To *draw* them close to me for comfort.

READER 3 (*speaking the female runner's line*). Just imagine finishing.

The actor playing the male runner strokes my hair gently, tucking a stray curl behind my ear.

ACTION: To *calm* my apparent nerves.

Alternatively:

READER 1. Let's run together.

The actor playing the female runner nudges me in the ribs.

ACTION: To *challenge* me before the race.

READER 2. I don't think I can do it.

I crush her foot underneath mine.

ACTION: To *undermine* her right from the start.

READER 3. Just imagine finishing.

The actor playing the male runner puts his arm firmly around the female runner.

ACTION: To *distance* me from them.

These actions may seem extraordinary in light of the situations; however, the given circumstances of the scene should justify them. Perhaps my character has been having an affair with the nurse throughout the play. He may even have tampered with the brakes on his girlfriend's car! Maybe my boss has had it in for me for some time, and didn't promote me, even though I was the best person for the job. The two other runners might have made a pact to win the race together.

Allow yourself to play with possible actions. Behaviour is often ambiguous and can be contradictory. We may do something but feel something entirely different. We may be talking to one person, but the intended target for what we are saying could be someone else.

The readers should allow any reactions to settle before the next line is spoken.

Skills

Analysis, Focus, Physicality

Responding to the Action

Repeat the exercise *Physicalising the Action* with a reader speaking the line and the actor playing the role making physical contact with someone in the scene.

This time, everyone in the scene behaves as though they are the main focus of the story. Each character will either say '*Better*' or '*Worse*' in reaction to what is being done and how it makes them feel. It is important to be physically dynamic when responding, so all the actors should embody their attitude to the actions that they are witnessing as well as saying whether it makes them feel better or worse.

For example, returning to the first scenario in the hospital, as my girlfriend covers my eyes I might pull away and say '*Worse*', witnessing how distressed she is. The actor playing the nurse might step forward and say '*Better*' because she is glad that her patient is addressing the situation with someone who loves her. Again, this will all be dependent on the given circumstances of the scene.

Skills

Analysis, Physicality, Responsiveness

Striking a Pose

All the actors should be aware of the given circumstances of the script. Play the scene. When the facilitator says '*Cheese!*', everyone freezes as though they are having their photograph taken.

As they freeze, the actors should physicalise the action that they are playing in order to accentuate it, highlighting what they are doing at that given point in time.

Let's imagine that the scene is at a picnic party. As they hear the word '*Cheese!*', one character poses hunched over the picnic cloth with a huge piece of cake stuffed in his mouth. His action is to *prevent* anyone else from getting to the food. Another lays her head in the lap of the man next to her. Her action is to *seduce* the host of the party. Another looks up anxiously for signs of rain. Her action is to *ensure* that everyone will have a good time. A fourth leans over to push the girl's head off the man's lap. Her action is to *deter* the girl from seducing her husband.

When the facilitator says '*Click!*', this will signify that the photograph has been taken and the scene can resume. The facilitator will say '*Cheese!*' and '*Click!*' throughout the course of the scene, and the actions will shift as the narrative unfolds.

This exercise serves to magnify the actions of the characters. Start with broad brushstrokes, but as the scene is repeated, the actions should be refined so that they are not so outwardly visible, but present nonetheless.

Skills

Analysis, Focus, Physicality

Interpreting the Action

Play the scene.

The character on the receiving end of an action asks what the person is trying to do to them with that action, using a transitive verb, something that is being *done* to them. For example they might say:

- *'Are you trying to seduce me?'*
- *'Are you trying to impress me?'*
- *'Are you trying to threaten me?'*

This is not about guessing the action correctly. There cannot be a right or a wrong. You may not be sure what is being done to you, but as long as you respond to what has just happened, it is valid.

It may be that an action is directed at one character, but is for the benefit of another person in the scene. In that case that person can also respond with a question that interprets the action: *'Are you trying to flatter/provoke/ostracise me?'*, etc.

Note

The purpose of this exercise is to ensure that not only are actions being played, but also that their recipient is responsive to the actions being directed towards them. The behaviour of characters will be altered by the nature of the questions asked.

Skills

Analysis, Awareness, Responsiveness

It's All About You

Repeat the exercise *Interpreting the Action*, but this time every character in the scene thinks that this is a story about them. They are the focus of each beat of the narrative. As a result, in response to each action *everyone* in the scene will simultaneously ask the question '*Are you trying to — me?*', substituting a suitable transitive verb for the dash.

What happens to your body in the space from your own egotistical viewpoint? Even your toes should have an opinion if you are fully engaged.

This exercise might require you to stop every so often to consider what your character perceives is happening to them in the scene. Discussion may very well be generated.

Skills

Analysis, Awareness, Responsiveness

Distractions

The following games serve to distract the actor from an overanalytic response to the text. By removing the focus from the words themselves, the actor should find a fresh impetus to speak them. All actors need to be off-book for this quintet of exercises.

Squashing the Speaker

The actors involved in the scene lie on the floor. Two people lie across each of them. If one of the players is particularly strong then they may require a third body on top of them.

The actors speak the text aloud, but at the same time are attempting to get up, dislodging the bodies that are holding them down.

Skills

Energy, Multitasking, Physicality

Piggy in the Middle

One actor stands between two other players who throw a ball to each other over the head of the actor in the centre.

The actor in the middle must try to catch the ball, but at the same time speak their lines. Obviously the players throwing the ball on either side are going to make it as difficult as possible for the ball to be intercepted.

+ A ball

Skills
Energy, Multitasking

78

TEXT

Intrusion

A circle of players surrounds the actor or actors who appear in the scene. The circle should be very tight, preventing those working in the middle from being able to move too much without risk of hurting themselves.

The actors speak the scene whilst those forming the circle push, jostle, pat and ruffle them.

Skills

Awareness, Multitasking, Physicality, Rhythm

Tasks

Play the scene, but at the same time each actor should undertake a task. The task should be simple but require some concentration.

For example, the actor might attempt to count a pile of coins. They might try to thread a needle. They might copy out a complex passage from a textbook. They might try to build a house of playing cards. The tasks can either be mimed or attempted for real.

At the same time as engaging with the task thoroughly and with the intention of accomplishing it, the actors must stay faithful to the text and also communicate actively with whomever it is they are talking to.

+ Small props

Skills

Communication, Multitasking, Responsiveness

The Need to Speak

The actors play the scene, facing each other, but at some distance apart. As they speak, the other players will hold their arms and legs, preventing them from moving towards the object of their speech.

The actors speaking should try and rid themselves of their human restraints as they endeavour to communicate the content of the scene.

Skills
Multitasking, Physicality

INDEX OF GAMES

SKILLS

NUMBERS REFER TO GAMES NOT PAGES

Conflict

Control

Coordination

Energy

Focus

Goal-seeking

Imagination

Inner Life

Multitasking

Physicality

Relaxation

Responsiveness

Rhythm

Status

ALPHABETICAL LIST

NUMBERS REFER TO GAMES NOT PAGES

NOTES

NOTES